D1531607

Murder
Talks Turkey

Murder
Talks Turkey

Deb Baker

MIDNIGHT INK
WOODBURY, MINNESOTA

First Edition
First Printing, 2008

Book design and format by Donna Burch
Cover design by Lisa Novak
Cover art © 2007 by Cathy Gendron
Editing by Connie Hill

Midnight Ink, an imprint of Llewellyn Publications

Library of Congress Cataloging-in-Publication Data:
Baker, Deb, 1953–.
  Murder talks turkey / Deb Baker. — 1st ed.
    p.   cm. — (A Yooper mystery; #3)
  ISBN: 978-0-7387-1225-3
  1. Johnson, Gertie (Fictitious character)—Fiction. 2. Grandmothers—Fiction.
  3. Upper Peninsula (Mich.)—Fiction. I. Title.
PS3602.A586M88   2008
813'.6—dc22   2007046244

Midnight Ink
Llewellyn Publications
2143 Wooddale Drive, Dept. 978-0-7387-1225-3
Woodbury, MN 55125-2989 USA
www.midnightinkbooks.com

Printed in the United States of America

ONE

Word for the Day
Boondoggle (BOON dahg'uhl) n.
A pointless project. Work of no value, done merely to appear
   busy.

Alternate Word
Icky (IK ee) adj.
Very distasteful; disgusting.

In the Michigan Upper Peninsula we love our guns. There's a
lot of talk about how the federal government is plotting to take
our weapons away. Nobody, but nobody, is going to get our guns,
even if it means burying most of them in the ground and taking a
final stand with our legs spread wide and our favorite firing power
nestled in our arms.

   I have a perfect example of why upstanding citizens need weapons. If I'd had a gun with me in the Stonely Credit Union, none

of this would have happened. I'd have had a bead on the masked bandit before he could say boo.

Instead of boo, he said, "Everybody freeze."

How original is that? He might as well have said, "Stick 'em up."

Michigan's tall conifers and wide stretches of unpopulated land must have had him thinking he was back in the Wild West.

He swept a quick glance over his hostages, and our eyes locked. I stared back at him through the round holes in the mask he wore.

I'd bet my bottom dollar I knew him. Around here everybody knows everybody.

My name is Gertie Johnson. I'm sixty-six years old with three grown kids—Heather, Star, and Blaze—all named after the horses I wanted but never had. My son, the local sheriff, is on temporary leave from work with a full-blown case of brain swell. And I don't mean that figuratively. He's recovering from bacterial meningitis. He went through a fight for his life before miraculously beating the odds. He should be in a rehabilitation center instead of home causing trouble, but he's half Swede and his wife is Finnish. You can't tell them anything.

If Blaze had deputized me like I wanted him to do, I could have worn the Glock I swiped from him on my hip in full view.

Instead, I was in line at the credit union, weaponless, waiting to cash my social security check and minding my own business. That's when the robber decided to hold up Stonely's small-town version of a bank. Just my luck, he'd pick now.

We all stared at the unexpected interloper while he waved his gun. It was one of the cheapest excuses for fire power I'd ever seen, but at close range it could still do plenty of damage to a person's internal organs.

I could see thin, hard lips through the mask hole.

"I SAID, everybody freeze! And I want to see empty hands up in the air, right eh?"

I heard people's belongings—key chains, wallets, and such—clatter to the floor as we reached for the ceiling, all pretty much in unison: a new teller from Trenary, the credit union manager, Ruthie from the Deer Horn Restaurant, Cora Mae, and me. Oh, and Pearl, who was right up by the teller getting her money counted out. She let out a squeal that almost pierced my eardrums, but she quit making noise when the gunman threatened to bop her with his pistol.

Pearl's cash was the first dough the robber took, stuffing it into a pillowcase he pulled out of his jacket pocket.

Just before the thief interrupted us, Cora Mae, my best friend and partner in the Trouble Buster Investigative Company, had been filling me in on the latest events regarding our first paid job. Since we were in a public place, we were careful to keep our client's identity and our mission top secret. We communicated in Cora Mae's version of code, although I didn't know it yet.

"Kitty's going to Hell," she said, before blowing an enormous bubble gum bubble.

Kitty acts as my occasional bodyguard when she's looking for an excuse to hang out, and she's the third partner in our investigative business. Kitty pulls goofy stunts every once in a while, but I never considered her fire and brimstone material.

"Since when did you get so judgmental?" I said, thinking of some of Cora Mae's more risqué adventures.

She sucked in the bubble and rolled her eyeballs to express frustration with me. Then she whispered, "I said Hell, but I meant Paradise."

"Ahhhh," I said, catching on, sort of.

In Michigan you can go to Hell or Paradise, depending on your mood. Or you can veer off from either location and visit Christmas, where you can gaze at the world's tallest Santa and decorated houses even at this time of year: mid-April, the first day of turkey hunting season.

I glanced at Ruthie, who was in front of us in line, to see if she was listening in, but she was busy greeting the manager, Dave Nenonen, who stood behind the new teller, watching her every move.

"Wait until we're in the truck to tell me the rest," I said, scowling while I tried to figure out what Cora Mae was really trying to convey. Apparently I hadn't had enough coffee this morning.

I was still scowling when the big dope stuck us up.

I risked a good look at him while he pushed Dave toward the back room. He was dressed like everybody else in Stonely—camouflage jacket, leather gloves, black winter ski mask.

The mask should have been a dead giveaway. While it can be a bit nippy in April, we generally don't wear face coverings when the temperature rises above freezing.

If we hadn't been yakking in line, someone might have noticed the seasonable mask faux pas.

Then I glanced down at his feet. The robber was either one of the dumbest criminals alive, or he was the craziest. Who wears bright orange high tops to rob a credit union?

Granted, orange is our favorite color in Stonely, but we don't wear it on our feet. Jackets, gloves, hats, orange suspender pants. But not orange boots and definitely not orange sneakers.

"Hurry up," the robber snapped at Dave. "And the rest of you…" he waved the gun. "My partner is outside, ya know? Anybody try anything and you'll be leaking blood on the pavement."

Pearl squealed.

Dave, tough guy that he is, trotted right over, sorted through a string of keys, pushed a few buttons, and gave the thief open access to the credit union's reserve cash. "Stay where you are," our captor said, head swinging to encompass everyone in the room. "Anybody move and my partner opens fire." The robber disappeared inside the vault.

He must have had Dave in his sights because the manager didn't move a single hair on his head, didn't even blink.

I glanced quickly out the window. Nothing unusual struck me, no movement at all other than a pickup truck going by on Highway M35. If he really had a partner outside, the guy was well hidden. While I had the chance, I eased my stun gun out of my purse.

Either the credit union manager or the teller must have pressed a button under the counter at some point, because when I glanced toward the window again, I saw Dickey Snell running in a crouch from an unmarked car. His backup of deputized locals arrived right behind him, squealing into the parking lot, making enough noise to wake a teenage boy on a Saturday morning.

The masked marauder was doomed, and he knew it, judging by the way he bolted out of the back room. He jumped behind the counter and tried to smash the drive-thru window with the butt of his gun. When that didn't work, he clocked the teller on her forehead instead. Her eyes rolled up until the whites showed, then she went over backward.

Someone yelled, "Everybody down," and it didn't come from the robber. It came from outside the building. In the Upper Peninsula, or the U.P., as we call it, "Everybody down" means only one thing when guns are involved.

Pearl screamed again, and we all hit the floor.

Cora Mae, a little slow on the dive, clonked me in the head with a black, strappy high heel. From my face-down position, I could see orange sneakers running this way and that in short, confused motions.

"Boondoggle," I muttered, surprising myself with the unconscious use of my word for the day. Usually I have to really work at finding the proper usage conditions. I couldn't believe how my mind sharpened in times of crisis.

This guy was about to find out how pointless his misguided project really was.

"Crap," our robber screamed, panic choking him up. "Shi—"

A bullet zinged into the building, busting out the front window and shattering my hope for a peaceful hostage negotiation. We'd never seen a real bank robbery in Stonely before. Dickey Snell, temporary sheriff until Blaze recovered, must be in his glory at the opportunity to fire at random. The fact that local residents were inside wasn't slowing him down one bit. Dickey tends to be over-anxious, and he's been known to lose his self-control in stressful situations.

The robber had to be from out of town. Otherwise he wouldn't have tried to hold up the credit union. Everybody in Stonely is armed for combat, every weapon is a stone's throw away, and worst of all, or best of all depending on what side of the armory you're on, every one of us can shoot a nickel off the top of a beer can.

I don't know why, but I was worried about the robber's future health. Dickey hadn't even given him the option of surrendering. I had my stun gun hidden from view and I was fully prepared to take him down without bloodshed.

Movement on top of the town hall across the street caught my eye. From my position on the floor, I had a direct view of the sky and rooftops. A man with a rifle appeared in my line of sight. He took aim.

"Hit the floor," I shouted to him, pulling hard on his pant leg while firing up the stun gun at the same time.

But I was too late.

I heard a bang, more glass shattering, then an eerie moment of quiet.

The robber dropped to the floor, his peashooter skidding and landing not two inches from my face. The sharpshooter on the town hall roof peered through his scope and sighted-in again just in case the first shot hadn't done the job. Before turning off the stun gun, I gave the shooter a football timeout sign with my hands. I didn't know if he saw me, but he didn't fire again.

Dickey Snell burst through the front entrance. I wanted to pick up the robber's measly pistol and put a round into Dickey's rear end for endangering upstanding citizens by handling the situation like he'd cornered Butch Cassidy.

No-Neck Sheedlo, his partner in crime fighting, stumbled in behind him, along with half the town. Cora Mae stood up and smoothed herself out. The rest of us did, too. We formed a circle around the dead robber. No question about it. He was gone. Even with the face mask, we all knew. The staring, blank eyes and the hole through his forehead cemented his fate.

Dickey pulled off the robber's mask, and we stared some more.

"Not from around here," No-Neck offered, shaking his big neckless noggin. "Anybody know this guy?"

"No, not, nope." Heads shook, mouths muttered.

"He's from the U.P.," I offered, saddened by the abrupt end of a life.

"Not with shoes like that, ya know?" someone said.

"Expound on that, Gertie." Dickey, the know-it-all college graduate, puffed himself up.

"He said, eh."

Everyone waited. Dickey dropped his arms to his waist to suggest impatience.

"Spit it out," No-Neck said. "He said what?"

"He said, eh. E.H." Did I have to spell everything out for them? "He said eh at the end of his sentence, like a Yooper. He talked like us."

Tourists from down state like to compare our speech to characters from the movie *Fargo*, but they're dead wrong. We have a very distinct pattern of speech in the Upper Peninsula, and this guy had it.

Everyone stared at me like I'd lost my mind. "We do," I insisted, "talk different." Was I the only one who could tell? Years ago I came to the U.P. with my Barney, so I'm still considered a transplant by the old timers. Most of the locals lived here their whole lives and haven't even traveled outside of our state borders.

"Well, he won't be saying eh anymore, eh?" someone in the back offered.

Dickey bent down and looked him over. He wasn't much to see. Scrawny, stubbly face, bushy brows, a scar on his cheek that looked like a dog bite that had required a few stitches.

"Nice shot," Dickey said. "Who did the shooting?" Nobody said anything. "It's okay to come forward," he said. "Whoever you are, you won't be incarcerated. You'll be exonerated. You might even be in line for a special medal for bravery. Speak up."

Muttering among the onlookers.

"Oh, come on," No-Neck said. "Somebody shot him."

"A guy on the town hall roof plugged him," I said. "He had a rifle with a scope. Dickey, I mean, Deputy Snell, who did you send up there?"

"I didn't send anybody to the roof." Dickey was getting hot.

Cora Mae had been eyeing up the men, contemplating her next victim. She isn't called the Black Widow for nothing. Cora Mae married and buried three husbands, and she's on the make for another one.

She stopped preening and said something significant. "The dead robber said he had a partner outside." She giggled nervously. "He wasn't dead when he said it."

"I didn't see anyone outside until the armed forces showed up," I said to the acting sheriff. "It had to be one of your men."

Dickey ran his hands through his greasy hair and readjusted his cat-hair encrusted green jacket. "Deputy Sheedlo, I want statements from everybody."

No-Neck rearranged the alleged witnesses and started taking statements. A moan from behind the counter reminded us that someone had been injured. The new teller rose, holding her forehead. I guessed this would be her last day on the job.

We have our share of emergency medical technicians in Stonely. The local men and some of the women like to join the volunteer fire department so they can play with the red trucks and long hoses, but you can't qualify without the proper credentials. The town's finest rushed over to offer their assistance.

While they were administering to the teller, Dickey picked up the pillowcase and opened it. He pulled out a package of bills and ripped off the paper surrounding it. His mouth fell open, which is where it is most of the time anyway.

"What's wrong?" I said, leaning over the pillowcase for a good look.

Dickey reached in and pulled out more of the contents, peeling each bundle apart. He flung them over his shoulder and pulled out some more.

Pearl's cash was at the bottom. The rest of the pillowcase was stuffed with Monopoly money.

TWO

"HE ROBBED THE CREDIT union," I said, rehashing the event with Cora Mae while we sat at her kitchen table drinking coffee and eating sugar doughnuts. "But he didn't take the bank's money. Why would anybody do that? Why risk prison to steal thirty bucks from Pearl, then fill the rest of the sack with play dollars?"

"What if Pearl was his target?" Cora Mae said. She's always brightest when she has her sights on a man. Right now, the pasture was empty, which explained her dense question.

I laughed. "Pearl's ninety years old. Who would hurt her? And why go to the bank with a gun just to steal thirty dollars from her?"

Cora Mae draped an old towel over my shoulders and clipped the ends together with a clothespin. "Pearl's been burning up the phone lines, telling her side of the story to anyone who'll listen," she said, mixing the color she was about to put on my head. "She claims she hit him with her purse. Did you see that happen?"

"Pearl probably thinks she did. Her mind isn't what it used to be. Fred should have been inside with us instead of waiting in the truck. He'd have handled the situation."

Fred, my police-trained German shepherd, raised his head from the floor when he heard his name. He looked at me with adoration in his eyes. Devil Fangs, as I used to call him, was a ten-ton black shepherd with red eyes and teeth made for ripping. When the cops retired him, he came to live with me. Give Fred a scent, and he can find anybody or anything. He's proved his worth ten times over.

I bit into another doughnut.

Cora Mae started griping about the red hair dye I chose.

"The first time your hair turned red was a mistake on my part," she said. "But why on earth do you want to keep on dying it red?"

I plopped a piece of sugar doughnut in my mouth and chewed on the question.

The truth of the matter was that the red hair changed my personality for the better. I used to be drab and lifeless, exactly like my gray-streaked hair. Now I have more pep and vigor. I wake up every day and look forward to whatever new adventure comes my way.

"Remember how I used to be before I went red, Cora Mae? Quiet and retiring?"

"No," Cora Mae said, squirting color on my head and splashing a dab of it too close to my eyes for comfort. "You never were like that. Not since I've known you. You've always been bold and bossy." Then she gave me an affectionate smile. "But you sure are fun."

Cora Mae and I have been friends for a long, long time. I was there when she buried her husbands in the Trenary Cemetery, and she helped me two years ago when I lost my Barney.

We are almost as tight as the black knit sweaters she likes to wear ever since she discovered how great her boobs look in Wonderbras.

I wiped around my eyes with the old towel and thought about the dead robber while Cora Mae worked the gooey mess into a lather on my head. I finished my doughnut.

Cora Mae checked the dye, then pulled off a pair of latex gloves. "There. Sit for awhile." She poured more coffee for each of us. "Kitty called from Paradise. Her car broke down."

"She's supposed to be following Tony Lento," I said. "Our first paying job and she goes for a joyride? Unbelievable. Tell her to turn around and head home once she gets the Lincoln fixed. She beats that car to death with her crazy driving."

Lyla Lento had hired the Trouble Busters after her husband forgot to come home one night and couldn't produce a plausible excuse. It was Kitty's turn to tail him. Since Kitty was halfway across the state, he'd been loose without supervision for the entire morning.

It's tough being the boss.

"She's waiting for them to fix her car," Cora Mae said. "The mechanic said it would be another hour or so. And for your information, she *was* following him."

"Is he alone?"

"He was, right before she lost him."

"Did she call Lyla before taking off?" Tony Lento's work took him out of town periodically. His wife had expressed reluctance to pay travel expenses.

"Lyla told Kitty to stick with him this time."

The timer went off. I rinsed my hair and towel dried it. "Looks good," I said, putting a lot of compliment in my voice.

Cora Mae humphed. "What are we getting paid for the Lento job? You're very closed-mouthed about the fee. I have to think you don't want to tell me."

"Of course we're getting paid," I said, dodging the question even though my friend would be ecstatic when she found out. However, Kitty might not be quite as enthusiastic if she learned that we were getting paid in trade. That meant free manicures for all three of us for one year at Lyla's beauty salon.

Since Kitty chews her nails down to the quick and mine chip and break, Cora Mae would be the only grateful beneficiary. But it was worth it for the referrals that were bound to come pouring in after we busted Lyla's husband.

"Tony Lento is one of Stonely's finest upstanding citizens," Cora Mae said. "Lyla must be going through her change. Tony would never cheat on her."

"Did you ever hear of a wolf in sheep's clothing?" I replied. Tony was fortyish, a handsome man with a constant grin that said he knew how terrific he was and he wanted to spread his greatness around.

"He's never looked twice at me. That's how I know." Cora Mae was three years younger than I was. At sixty-three she looked like a million bucks. She eats nothing but salads and wears slinky black pumps and tight tops that display her perky Wonderbra-ed boobs. Every man in Tamarack County notices Cora Mae.

"No way," I said in disbelief. "He *had* to take a look at you."

"Not a one."

"Ever?"

"Never."

It was good to know that Cora Mae had one holdout. Two, if you counted George. But that sweet man was a daydream for another time. Right now we had work to do.

I had to figure out how to reconnect with Tony Lento somehow. And Kitty would have to explain to his wife why she lost him. Until she returned from Paradise, I had time on my hands. Cora Mae slithered down the road to her house. I hopped into the Trouble Buster truck with Fred and headed for the jail. Hopefully, Dickey Snell had some answers by now.

THREE

I KNOW TROUBLE WHEN I see it. Blaze's family car was parked behind Ray's General Store, next to the small jail building. My son hadn't been cleared for driving yet. Our family didn't know if he'd ever work again, let alone drive a vehicle. He hasn't been the same since the day he woke up in the hospital's ICU. After over a week on a respirator without blinking an eye, he'd beat the meningitis at its own deadly game. But he wasn't the same man. His recovery was slower than the syrup dripping from a maple tree tapped before its time.

Blaze was hunkered over in a chair with a handheld radio tight between his knees. "I need backup," he said into it, speaking in a whisper with his lips pressed against the transmitter.

"What are you doing here?" I demanded. He didn't even look up.

The radio crackled and a voice said, "Who's playing games on the emergency frequency? If you can't state your position or your problem, get off."

16

"This *is* an emergency," Blaze said. "I'm behind enemy lines. I need help getting out."

"Repeat. What's your position?"

"Blaze," I said. "Give me the radio."

He noticed me for the first time. "Oh, Ma, you're alive. Wait a minute. What are you doing here? There are Viet Cong everywhere." He clunked his head with a beefy palm. "Oh, Jesus, they captured you, too!"

Blaze had that look in his eyes, the one he gets when his infected brain starts playing tricks on him. Meningitis, our family has learned the hard way, is one of the scariest diseases on the planet. If it doesn't kill you outright, it robs you of your ability to tell fact from fiction. Blaze spends part of every day in the past, sliding through rice paddies on his belly, fighting for his life, and searching for a way to escape.

That's one of the reasons why his wife Mary stripped the house of weapons. It's why I kept his Glock.

Blaze moaned like it was the end of the world, but he let me take the radio from him. I turned it off. "See those keys?" I pointed to his car keys lying on the desk on the other side of his big body. "Hand them to me. We're going to bust out of here and Fred's going to help."

"If they catch us, we're dead." His gaze slid to Fred, who was eye level with my seated son. "What the hell is that animal?"

"You know Fred. He's my dog."

Blaze scowled, searching his brain.

Just then, Dickey opened the jailhouse door. Fred has good instincts so he growled. Even showed enough incisor to cause Dickey to take a step back. I patted my dog on the head, praising him for his smarts. "Good Boy."

"Why does he have to growl at me?" Dickey wanted to know. "I used to own him."

"Maybe that's why," I pointed out.

"Did any of them see you coming in?" Blaze said. "They'll torture us if they find out."

Dickey glanced sharply at me.

"We're Vietnam POWs," I explained. My heart ached for my son. You'd think one round of duty would be enough for one man to bear without having to revisit the war as many times as Blaze has. I hated to see him this way.

"I need to talk to Dickey," I said to Blaze. "Then we'll go turkey hunting." That was a lie, but it calmed him down. Yeah, right. Like I'd be caught dead out in the woods with an armed mental problem.

"You know I dislike being called Dickey," Dickey said. "If you can't address me properly and respectfully as Deputy Snell, at least refer to me as Dick."

"I wiped your hinder when you were a baby," I reminded him. "You'll always be Dickey to me."

"Hand me the twelve-gauge shotgun on the rack," Blaze said, pointing at the jail cell, which obviously didn't include a line of firearms. "I'm going to polish it up before we go."

"Not right now, son." I shifted my attention back to Dickey, who hung his hat on a hook and ran his hands through his hair. Dickey Snell was skinny as a pole, but he made up for it in strut. He had played cops and robbers since he was old enough to walk, and he took the job seriously. No monkey business. Rules and regulations were sacred, whether or not they made any sense.

"You have to keep Blaze out of the office," he said, watching Blaze fiddle with a ball of fuzz he'd picked off his sweater. "This is the fourth incident."

"It's like home to him," I said. "Lighten up. Did you figure out who the robber was?"

"Kent Miller from the Soo."

"Our side of the water?"

He nodded.

Sault Ste. Marie, or The Soo as we call it, is at the northeasternmost tip of the Michigan Upper Peninsula and is connected by a bridge to its twin city on the Canadian side. Pronounced Su Saint Marie (not Salt Sty Marie), it's home to the Soo Locks and is located a good two, two and a half hours, from Stonely.

"What else?" I asked.

"His wallet was in his pants, he didn't have any priors, and he was the worst bank robber I've ever seen."

As though Dickey had any experience with armed robbers. I could have yanked Dickey's chain by saying that Miller *was* the worst robber, because the Stonely cops managed to catch him, but I kept quiet. I'm not one to cause a stir.

"Who shot him?" I said after a reasonable time, when Dickey didn't offer it up.

Dickey straightened the lapels on his green jacket. "That's yet to be ascertained. You're the only one who witnessed the shooter."

"I was on the floor of the credit union," I said. "The guy on the roof wore the same kind of clothes we all wear." I glanced at Dickey's Joe Friday clothes. "The same as most of us, anyway. Jeans, brown jacket with a big hood bunched up at the back of his neck, black gloves."

"Did you see his face?"

I sighed and thought back. "He was across the street, too far away for facial details."

"Well?"

"I'm thinking. Let me think." I snapped my fingers. "Okay, I know. He was wearing a black Kromer."

Dickey glared at me. "That's your contribution? A Kromer? Everybody in the U.P. owns one."

I glared back. "You now have more information than you had before. You can't even keep your deputies under control or you'd know who it was. You're lucky to have what I just gave you."

"A Kromer." Dickey shook his head.

A Kromer is a special hat designed by George "Stormy" Kromer, a railroad engineer who lost his hat so many times he modified an old baseball cap with earbands that wrapped around the sides of the cap and tied in the front. In cold or windy conditions, the bands could be untied, wrapped around the ears, and tied under the chin. Michigan loggers and hunters have been wearing them for years.

"Which one of your Keystone cops," I fairly shouted at Dickey, "was wearing a Kromer?"

"I'll continue to interrogate residents until I find out."

Fred sat down on my foot. With a little effort, I pulled it out. "How's the teller?"

"An ambulance transported her to Escanaba. The hospital is keeping her overnight for observation. She's the one who sounded the alarm."

This Kent Miller really was a dumb bank robber. Not only did he have identification in his pocket and orange sneakers on his feet, he left the teller behind the counter with the alarm button, and he filled his pillowcase with play money.

"What's the teller's name?" I asked.

"Mrs. Johnson, this is official law enforcement work. Please take your son and your old dog home."

Fred stared at Dickey, and a soft but audible growl tickled his throat. What a dog!

"I'd like to send flowers to the injured woman," I punted. "I need her name to do that. If you won't tell me, I'll have to talk to someone in the emergency room."

Dickey pulled a notebook out of his pocket and flipped through it with a sigh. "Angie Gates," he said.

"The case is closed, right?" I asked. If Blaze had been well and handling the case, he'd be all done. The distant glare of retirement had blinded my son, and he put most of his energy into making it to the social security line without breaking a sweat.

"An outside auditor is ascertaining the credit union's cash. I demanded a full accounting. This investigation isn't over until I have all the pertinent facts and feel comfortable with those facts." I have to say this for Dickey, he didn't give up easily. There was more to learn than we knew at the moment. I was sure of it.

Fred plopped his head on the desk, causing Blaze to leap from the chair. "Get me a rifle! There's a bear in here."

"Time to go," I said, steering Blaze out the door, to my truck, and coaxing him in. Fred rode in the back bed to keep my son from overreacting. We drove through our small town, headed south, and turned, passing my house and following the gravel road that led to Blaze's trailer home.

His wife Mary was at the kitchen table, sobbing her eyes out.

"What did they take?" Blaze demanded, when he saw her. "I knew it. The minute I turned my back. Did they get the money?"

"I can't take it one more minute," Mary sputtered. "He wanders around day and night. I can't keep track of him."

Blaze stormed down the hall.

"He'll be back in a minute," she said, "telling us someone stole his money."

"Someone stole my five million dollars," Blaze hollered.

"I moved the hiding place," Mary shouted back, then turned to me with sad, puppy dog eyes. "See? It was a mistake to bring him home so soon."

"He's better than he was," I said.

"That's not saying much."

"All you need is a good night's sleep," I suggested. "Why don't you go visit your daughter at college? Go away for a few days and rest. I'll take Blaze home with me."

What was I saying? I could hardly handle what I had, let alone watch over my son.

Mary sniffed. "Really?" Her eyes shone with hope.

"Go pack," I said to her back end.

She was already running down the hall.

FOUR

GRANDMA JOHNSON ATTEMPTED TO heat up frozen pasties while I was gone. How many times have I asked her to stay out of the kitchen? A hundred times, at least, and that's just this week.

Grandma is my ninety-two-year-old mother-in-law. After Barney died, I went through a typical grieving process, starting with anger and moving slowly through despair. Two years later, I'm still angry with him for leaving me alone to deal with his mother.

The worst part is, she moved in with me, and I can't get rid of her. It's still a mystery why she picked me, since we've never gotten along. Personally? I think she's plotting to drive me insane.

" 'Bout time you showed up," she snapped "The oven is broken." She pointed at the dishwasher. "My pasties are wet and soggy. Ruined!"

Grandma has been known to serve raw chicken to a table of guests. And she's been known to blow out the stove's pilot light and turn the burners on, causing deadly fumes to waft through the house. My home is going to explode one of these days, if I don't get her into a nursing home.

"I'll fix it," Blaze offered, bending and squinting at the dishwasher. "Where's the chain saw?"

"What are you doing here?" Grandma Johnson said. "I thought you were in a POW camp."

Barney's mother has hardening of the brain arteries, just enough to be dangerous. The next several days of living with her and Blaze would be more exciting than I could possibly handle.

"Cora Mae," I said into the phone, after I had deposited the two kooks at the kitchen table with canned chicken noodle soup and saltines. Grandma was right for a change. The pasties hadn't been dishwasher safe. They were ruined. "Can you come and stay with me? It'll only be a couple days."

"Fat chance," my best friend said. "I know you have Blaze over there."

"How did you find out?"

"Scanner. Blaze announced it over the airwaves."

I turned around and sure enough, he was in the next room on the radio, whispering coordinates to some imaginary ally. The police scanner Cora Mae gave me last year popped and crackled. We stopped talking on both ends of the phone line and listened in. I recognized Dickey Snell's voice. He puffed and pontificated and coded this and ten-somethinged that. "That's Blaze Johnson compromising the emergency channel. Can someone remove him from the radio?"

Once Cora Mae and I realized Dickey had nothing useful to say we went back to business.

"I can't come over," Cora Mae continued, "but Kitty's back and—"

"I'll be right there," I heard Kitty shout from Cora Mae's side of the phone.

Within minutes she was slamming through the front door. "Tony Lento got away from me this side of Paradise," Kitty said, making herself at home at the kitchen table next to Grandma Johnson and Blaze, who had returned to his chair for more army rations.

"Hell," Blaze said, picking at a cracker.

"No, I said Paradise," Kitty answered.

"I like Climax best," Grandma Johnson said, forgetting her table manners. She giggled.

"That's under the bridge," Kitty reminded her. "Quite a ways from Paradise."

"What was Tony doing in Paradise?" I asked.

"Business, I guess. You're next up to watch him. His wife says he's going turkey hunting in the morning."

"Lyla took me over behind Bear Creek. He has a ground blind set up."

"Do you want company?"

"I'll manage as long as you can watch Blaze and Grandma."

"It must be icky for you, taking care of these two alone," Kitty said, using the alternate word for the day, falling right into my trap.

———

Icky!

I laughed out loud all the way to Escanaba. Kitty and I were in a big-word contest. She had a way of infiltrating my word of the day notes to discover my next word and then flaunting her assumed superior vocabulary abilities in my face by using the word first. Or, she'd use a humongous word and expect me to challenge her with an even larger word.

Those days are over. I made a "mistake" and left this week's words where she could easily find them. However, she has her mitts on the alternate list, which is nothing like the real word list. Icky was today's alternate word.

The last thing I said to her before I left her in charge of Blaze and Grandma was, "Boondoggle."

"What are friends for?" she replied, looking a trifle confused.

I turned onto Ludington Street, parked the truck, and swung through the hospital's revolving door. The gift shop was still open, so I purchased a small display of flowers, asked for Angie Gates' room number, and took the elevator up.

She was asleep. I cleared my throat loud enough to wake her up and placed the flowers on her bed stand, busying myself with the arrangement while she blinked away the sandman.

"You were at the credit union this morning," Angie said, her voice gravely. She scooted up into a sitting position, grimacing with pain and gingerly touching her head. "Thanks for the flowers."

Angie Gates was a hard-baked thirty or thirty-five year old. Although she was pretty enough, she'd smoked and partied too much, and it showed. I've seen that a lot, people adrift, waiting out their time on earth to pass, trying to rush the end.

"How are you doing?" I asked. "That was quite a clonk to your head."

"Concussion," she said. "I'm quitting that job the minute I'm released."

"Tough break. We never had a robbery before."

"I didn't like the work much anyway. I'm going back to wait-ressing. I can make more in tips in one day than I can all week counting out money that isn't mine."

"I wish you'd reconsider. Give it another chance." I felt bad for the woman.

A nurse came in and fussed over Angie, taking her blood pressure and temperature and checking the IV. When she left the room, I said, "The robber's name was Kent Miller."

"Never heard of him, but I've only been in the U.P. about a year."

"He was from the Soo. No one around here knew him. The pillowcase was full of Monopoly money."

"I heard."

"What do you make of that?"

Angie shrugged. "Someone was trying to cover up something."

"A cover up?" I hadn't thought of that.

"Sure. I saw it on TV. The money's already gone due to an inside job, and the pressure's on to account for it, so the real thief plans a robbery that isn't really a robbery. In the television show, the fake robber got away."

I thought over Angie's theory and decided it had merit. If she ever wanted to work for manicures instead of money, I'd hire her in a minute.

"Who'd do a thing like that?" I asked. The credit union staff had been entrenched in Tamarack County forever. Except Angie. But she had sounded the alarm. Aside from Dave Nenonen, who managed the business, the only other employees besides Angie were two part-timers—Dave's wife and June Hopala. June worked to supplement her social security. Both the Nenonens and the Ho-palas went way back.

Angie must have thought my question was rhetorical, because she didn't answer. Rhetorical was my word for tomorrow. I was one step ahead of myself, and I felt proud that I was doing my thinking in higher language.

"I heard you saved the day," I said.

"I should get a medal for bravery," she said, somewhat sarcastically. "Fat lot of good it did me. All I have to show for my effort is a big knot on my head and a huge hospital bill."

"The credit union should pay your bills."

She snorted like she didn't believe it.

I drove home from the hospital with the pretend robbery theory rifling through my thoughts. But the credit union robbery wasn't even my problem. Let Dickey figure it out. Tomorrow I would be on a surveillance run, tailing Tony Lento. The Trouble Busters had to bust this guy and prove our worth, if we wanted to stay in business.

FIVE

Word for the Day
Rhetorical (ri 'tor i KL) n.
A question to which no answer is expected.

Alternate Word
Ereption (E rep tion) n.
Snatching away.

I POSITIONED MYSELF OUT of range, behind a large maple tree. The rules of safe turkey hunting were like the facts of life to me. Stay one hundred yards away from another hunter, don't use a gobbler call unless you want hunters to show up instead of turkeys, and never wear red, white, or blue clothes. Those are the primary colors of a gobbler's head. Save the patriotic garb for the Fourth of July parade or you won't be home for supper.

The American wild turkey is the most difficult game in North America to hunt. That's according to the Michigan DNR's hunting guide. Turkeys have eyes, ears, and a sense of awareness that is ten times faster and better than anything we humans have.

And, believe it or not, they really can fly. How else would they dodge night predators? They roost in trees in great big extended-family flocks. Depending on the time of year, turkeys congregate in hen flocks, bachelor flocks, and mating flocks.

Turkey season was in high gear, but I hadn't heard one shot yet this morning. The turkeys must be holed up safe and sound, while watching the calendar for the end of hunting season.

I chose a tree with a substantial trunk to hide every last part of my body from view. I wore camo, so I blended in, and thick gloves and boots because our April mornings can be a "mite" chilly. The outdoor thermometer registered a brisk thirty-six degrees when I left home, creeping out undetected. Kitty never missed a snore from the couch, and Grandma and Blaze were still bedded down.

Tony Lento should be arriving any minute.

I could see my breath in the cold air, so I covered my mouth with my glove when I peeked out to watch Tony's spot. Lyla had walked me out here when she hired the Trouble Busters and assured me that Tony would be behind bales of straw some hundred yards away from the tree I hid behind. He hunted every morning, she'd said, like clockwork.

My job was to find out what species he was hunting.

Lyla had sworn me to secrecy. A private investigator has to be discrete. We wouldn't stay in business long if our clients couldn't trust us. So the rule was, no telling anyone outside of the three partners. No telling now and no telling later. While I waited, I worried about Kitty's blabbermouth. Our lips were supposed to be sealed till our deaths, and if Kitty couldn't keep it reined in, she'd make a quick departure from this world.

Which is what I promised her, if she whispered one word about our client to anyone.

There isn't a turkey flock in the U.P. as large as Kitty's hen flock. She's the queen hen because she knows more good gossip than anyone else in Tamarack County.

Kitty rules her roost of biddies from a formidable physique. She wears a bunch of pincurls in her gray hair, rarely combing them out, and she's built like a semi. That's why she makes the perfect bodyguard when I get into trouble, or when I need her to watch over my kooky family.

A branch snapped to my left, and I almost let out a yelp. Good thing I was nearly frozen to death, or I might have screeched. Another branch broke. Leaves shuffled under someone's heavy boots. Any turkey worth half his salt was in the next county by now.

I cautiously eased one eye out from behind the tree to get a good look at Tony's makeshift turkey blind.

A mean, snarky, green-uniformed creep named Rolly Akkala glared back at me from the straw bales.

"What the hell are you doing behind that tree?" the local game warden asked. "Why aren't you in your own blind? Come out here. Lord, I hate this job. You nearly scared me to death."

His demise would make all of Stonely happy enough to throw a party at Herb's Bar. A Rolly Akkala's Bit the Dust party would draw more revelers than a Packers versus Lions football game.

I popped out from behind the maple. My cover was blown, thanks to the warden. Rolly walked toward me. He had tree-stump legs, a barrel chest, and a jaw like a bulldog.

31

"Cough it up," he said, holding out his hand.

"What?"

"Turkey license." He snapped his fingers two times then extended his hand, palm up. "Let's see it."

"I don't have a license," I said. "I'm not hunting."

I was hunting all right but not for the feathered kind of turkey. Rolly rolled his eyes. "I've heard that one before."

"I'm really not." I spread my arms wide. "Do you see a gun?"

"Just in case you get any ideas, I've got one right here on my side," our warden said, tapping his holster. "Good thing, too, with the likes of you hunting illegally." He walked around the maple tree, parting brush with his foot. "Your weapon's around here someplace. Put your hands up against the tree and no monkey business."

Just then Tony Lento walked into our friendly gathering. "What's going on?" he said. Tony carried a shotgun under his arm and his standard I'm-a-great-guy grin.

"I don't need to look at yours, Mr. Lento. I'm sure you're within the law."

"Well, Rolly," Tony said. "I have it right here. Take a look anyway." He held out his turkey hunting license. "Everybody should be treated the same. Hello, Gertie."

"Hi, Tony."

"Didn't I tell you to put your hands up against that tree?" Rolly said to me. "Help me search the ground for her weapon, Mr. Lento, and shoot her if she moves."

By the time the surrounding woods and my physical person had been thoroughly searched by the warden, half the day was gone.

Not only that, Tony had given up on getting a good shot after the brouhaha with Rolly. He'd chucked it in for the rest of today, leaving me hugging the tree, unable to follow after him.

Someday, someone is going to clean that warden's clock.

After Rolly satisfied himself that I wasn't armed, I traipsed out of the backwoods—cold, hungry, and having lost my man.

———

Grandma Johnson sat at the kitchen table having coffee with her friend Pearl, who claimed she had saved us at the credit union by whacking the robber with her purse to give the rescuers a clear shot. She was experiencing a bit of fame among the old-age set and she wasn't about to miss the opportunity.

Fred had been banished to the great outdoors. He and Grandma don't see eye to eye, which is all the more reason for me to like my dog. He came inside with me, all ten tons of black hair and red eyes. Pearl squealed. So did Grandma. "Get that thing outta the house," she said.

"Where is Kitty?" I swung my head. Fred plopped down by the door, ready to bolt if Grandma grabbed the fly swatter. "And where's Blaze?"

"That lippy friend of yours took Blaze along to the sheriff's station." Grandma clacked her false teeth in agitation. "Don't send her over to babysit me no more."

"She wasn't here to take care of you," I said. "She was here to make Blaze comfortable." Who would want to keep this old battle axe safe from harm? If she tried to stick her fingernail file into a light socket, I wouldn't say a word to stop her.

Pearl piped up, "Blaze said they stole the money."

"Blaze has a few mental problems," I said.

"Says who?" Grandma asked, staring at me with eyes beadier than Fred's.

"Says the doctors. He thinks he has millions stashed away, and thieves are after it."

"He told me about that," Pearl said. "Such a shame. But this is different money. This news came from one of the deputies."

"Never did like that Dickey Snell," Grandma said, stating the only fact we've ever agreed on. "Gertie's going to drive us over to Trenary for bingo tonight. Now that she has her driver's license."

"That's an easy one to get," Pearl said.

"Took her long enough," Grandma said.

I haven't informed my mother-in-law of my status, because she doesn't need to know everything about my personal life. After enough crabbing and threatening from Blaze, I went to Escanaba and passed my written test. I'm official now. Except, I'm supposed to have a fully licensed driver in the car with me at all times. The rules they make! I have a temporary license for six months, then I get the real one.

"What did Dickey say?" I asked, still wondering about Kitty and Blaze. Kitty knew better than to take Blaze down to the sheriff's office. What if something important was happening?

"The money's missing," Pearl said again. "It's gone."

"Serves Blaze right," Grandma said, picking up her cup from a pool of spilled coffee and taking a drink.

"I'm not talking about Blaze's hidden fortune," Pearl said, slurping coffee between words. "By the way, I hope Blaze is right. A millionaire! In Stonely! Imagine that. But I'm trying to tell you that the credit union money is missing."

"That's impossible," I said. "There was only one robber and he had a pillowcase filled with play money."

"And he had my hard-earned cash," Pearl said. "Don't forget that. It's why I clocked him with my purse." Pearl did a swinging motion, a re-enactment of events before continuing. "A hundred thousand. That's what Deputy Snell said. All missing."

"Serves 'em all right," Grandma said.

"Come on, Fred." I grabbed Fred's leash from a hook by the door and hurried out with him at my side.

Something had happened, and I was missing it.

SIX

"LET HER OUT," DICKEY said to Blaze when I slipped into the sheriff's office. Fred howled from the truck, which is what he always does when I leave him behind. He sounded like an entire wolf pack.

Kitty, pin curls and all, sat on a cot behind the jail bars. "Why did you let him lock you up?" I wanted to know.

"It seemed easier than fist fighting with him," she replied. "I planned on defending myself only if he got out a rope and started making a noose."

"Release her this moment." Dickey was puffing up like a Tom turkey.

Blaze jiggled the keys and leaned back in the sheriff's chair. "She broke the speed limit on the way over. Probably broke the speed of sound, if that's possible. She's a menace to society, and she's staying locked up until traffic court convenes."

Sounded good to me. Kitty liked to blow through town like a tornado, taking corners on two wheels, and practicing other tomfoolery usually reserved for delinquent teenagers. I gripped the bars and pressed my face against the cold steel. "Anything rhetorical to say about your situation?" I said to her, using my word for the day.

"We need an ereption of those keys," Kitty said, using hers. Badly, I might add.

"You quit that foul talk," Blaze shouted. "Or I'll keep you locked up for the rest of the week. I'll throw away the key."

I grinned. "Could you repeat that, Kitty? I didn't quite hear you."

Kitty swung her eyes at Blaze, then whispered, "Get me out of here. Please."

"In a minute," I said, turning to Dickey. "I heard money is missing from the credit union."

Our stand-in sheriff nodded his head. "A significant amount of money has been taken."

"How do you account for that? The robber was stopped dead in his tracks."

"An accomplice."

"The guy was in the bank alone."

"An inside job."

Dickey Snell had figured that out on his own. Amazing. College boys are known for big words, not common sense. Blaze must have helped him with that deduction.

The howling outside subsided.

"The next time I find Blaze inside this facility," Dickey said. "I'm putting him behind bars for trespassing."

"You do that," I replied, looking tough, "and you'll have me to answer to."

Dickey snorted.

"Remember me," Kitty called from behind bars. "I have to go, you know, and I'm not using this open—"

"Okay," I said. "Blaze, give me the keys and I'll watch her. You have to check out your house."

"Why do I have to do that?"

"You know why." I made the universal money sign by rubbing my thumb across my fingers to remind him of his hidden millions. "You have to make sure it's all accounted for. I'll drive you over."

Blaze caught my drift and bolted for the door, tossing the keys at me. I hated to see the look of concern on his face, but short of wrestling him to the ground, it was the only way.

Before I let Kitty out, I made her say ereption six times as fast as she could. "That was for doing such a poor job of watching my son," I said.

"This is your last official warning," Dickey said. "Keep him home."

———

Hunting seasons always remind me of my Milwaukee grandson, Little Donny, because he usually comes for every one of them. He loves the wildness of our land and he fits in well with the people here, even though he's had some unusual experiences and hasn't managed to shoot anything.

One time, Little Donny stunned a buck and loaded him in Carl's station wagon. Then the buck woke up. What a mess that made of Carl's wagon before we got the car door open and let the deer run off.

Nineteen-year-old Little Donny has a new job in Milwaukee so he can't get time off to turkey hunt this year. I really miss him.

I named my kids for the horses I never had, but always dreamed of having. Blaze, Star, and Heather. The girls like their names, but Blaze has a little residual resentment over his. Heather lives in Milwaukee and Star lives just down our road behind me. She's my youngest and has twin boys, Red and Ed, who own Herb's bar, the only watering hole in Stonely.

I'd promised Kitty a reprieve from her daycare duties, and I knew just what to do to accomplish my mission without compromising my sleuthing schedule. I walked into the tavern, noting that the four o'clock crowd had arrived ahead of me. The bar went dead silent when I stepped in, but conversations resumed as soon as they saw it was only me.

Star was behind the bar with Red, who was named for his brilliant shock of red hair.

"I need help," I said to Star after she plunked a diet pop down in front of me. "Mary's gone for a few days and I can't handle my new business and take care of Grandma and Blaze at the same time."

"I get off in thirty minutes, I'll come over."

I sighed with relief.

"I'm off tomorrow," she continued, "I'll do it then, too."

"You're the best."

"I know," Star said, with a twinkle in her eye, which left me pondering what she meant by that remark. Star's husband ran off several years ago and she's been playing the field ever since. My baby is cute and cuddly and I miss spending time with her. Between helping the boys keep Herb's bar running and her active social life, I don't see much of my daughter.

I drank my pop, then headed home to wait for Star to get off work.

———

"What do you mean, you lost him?" Cora Mae said from her kitchen table as the sun set in orange stripes outside the window.

"It's harder than it sounds," I said, digging into the platter of pan-fried chicken Kitty had made on Cora Mae's little-used stovetop. "It might help if you could drive. Kitty and I are doing all the surveillance work."

"You can practice with me," Kitty offered, licking her fingers. "You had your license at one time, so you must know how. You're just rusty."

"I better start right now," Cora Mae said. "Because you and Gertie are doing an awful job of tailing him."

That was the truth, but I hated to admit it. "That's not true," I said.

Cora Mae used her fingers to pop one measly piece of lettuce into her mouth from the salad in front of her. "I've been doing research while you two have been busy losing Tony."

"You found out who he's seeing on the side?" Kitty asked.

"No. I found out about the orange sneakers on the bank robber."

"We should look into that case, too," I said. "Since I was one of the hostages, I'm interested."

"Nothing could keep you away from a case like this," Kitty said. "Even if you hadn't been in the credit union when it happened."

Cora Mae ate another bit of lettuce. "Kent Miller came from the Soo, that's his legal address, but he was trying to break into a gang."

"Imagine applying for a gang position. Is that how it's done?" I said. "And what are they called? The orange shoe gang?"

"That's their logo, or whatever a gang calls its individual mark."

Kitty rolled a mouthful of chicken into one cheek. "He's a gang-banger? Wow. A gangbanger right in our backyard."

"An amateur one," I reminded her. "A real one would have shot all of us."

Kitty tackled another piece of chicken. "Why would he announce himself that way?"

"He never expected to get caught. Gang members aren't very smart," I guessed with some confidence. Not that Stonely ever had a gang. The closest we came was two years ago when Jesse Olson and his gang took baseball bats and beat up all the local mailboxes in broad daylight. That gang wasn't too bright, either.

"It's an inside job," I said. "His accomplice has to be Dave Nenonen. He's the manager, so he's the only one with total access to the cash. And you should have seen how hot he was to open the vault. Didn't put up a fuss at all."

Kitty nodded. "Maybe Dave siphoned out the money over time and the robbery was intended to draw attention away from him."

"Dave's like family," Cora Mae said. "He's not our guy."

Every man in town is like family to Cora Mae. She's dated almost all of them and doesn't have a mean word to say about a single one.

Before Dave married Sue and while Cora Mae was between husbands, they had a little fling. When they meet here and there in
town, I can't help noticing that Dave won't look Cora Mae directly
in the eye. Like if he did, he'd remember something so special, he'd
lose control of his married life.

That's what Cora Mae does to a man.

Tonight, after nibbling her few crumbs of rabbit food, she
dressed all in black—dainty boots, tight black jeans, and a soft and
fuzzy sweater with glitter. Kitty wore a housedress tent thing and
had combed out all but a row of pin curls in the front.

"You still have pin curls in your hair." I thought I should mention it in case she had missed them.

"I know," the beauty queen answered, without offering an explanation. "How's it going with you and George?"

I'm a recent widow, so George and I are taking it slow at my
request. George has been a family friend for as long as I can remember. He's sixty years old and can fix anything that's broken.
The two of us are like soul mates. To top it off, he has tight buns
and great muscles in all the right places.

"He'll be along later," I said. "He's finishing a carpentry job."

Since Star was babysitting Blaze and Grandma, and had agreed to
take them to play bingo, the three of us had free rein to handle business. The big occasion that had Kitty doing a comb out was the spring
dance in Trenary. It was held in the senior center, next to the church
that hosted the bingo games that Grandma and Pearl were going to.

Friday night dances in the U.P. aren't as filled with excitement
as non-Yoopers might think. However, all the locals would be

there, including Tony and Dave. We could pick up a lost trail and question Dave at the same time. Kill two birds with one stone.

As it turned out, only one bird died, and it wasn't either of those two boys.

SEVEN

Trenary, with five hundred residents, is a big city compared to Stonely. It has a few bars, a grocery store, a pizza place, and the cemetery where my Barney is buried. It's also home to the U.P.'s famous Trenary toast, a Finnish cinnamon treat sold in a brown paper bag. We love strong coffee, and we love to dip Trenary toast into it.

If it were daylight, Cora Mae and I would have stopped at the cemetery and visited her three deceased husbands, who managed to get buried together in one plot with room left over for Cora Mae someday. I often wonder what they would have thought of their final interment arrangement.

Barney's waiting on me too, but I'm not nearly ready to leave this world—although I miss him so much, I have a permanent ache in my heart.

The drive to Trenary was slow going. I followed Kitty's car in the Trouble Buster truck, which used to belong to Blaze before the department bought him a new truck and put this one on the auction block. I nabbed it for a song. The best part of the deal was the lights and sirens were still in good working order.

Cora Mae swerved down US 41 like a drunken sailor. Kitty had to be scared near to death sitting in the passenger seat next to her. Driving isn't going to be one of Cora Mae's top abilities, but to be fair, I had a couple of incidents when I started to drive. In fact, I rolled my Barney's truck into a ditch and totaled it.

I'm such a good driver now, I can multitask while steering. Reaching under the seat, I pulled out my Glock and caressed it. I'd always wanted one, and here it was, resting on my lap. I considered putting it in my purse for the dance, but reluctantly rejected the idea as a bad accident waiting to happen.

Cora Mae steered right at a ditch, then overcorrected and headed toward the other side of the median. I returned the Glock to the floor, turned on the truck's lights and siren, and forced Cora Mae to a stop on the side of the road.

"Kitty," I said, after stomping around the front of our vehicles and wrenching open the passenger door. "I'm going to have a heart attack watching this. Let's teach Cora Mae to drive another time when we aren't in a hurry. The dance will be over before we get there."

"I'm just starting to get the hang of it," Driving Momma said with some defensive huff in her voice.

"We're out on the highway, and you're going fifteen miles an hour in a sorry excuse for a straight line."

Kitty's curls bobbed to the beat while she came around the car and traded places with Cora Mae.

In spite of the initial delays, we made it to the dance in record time. Kitty's hot foot led the way, while my truck's lights and sirens cleared a path right down the middle of US 41.

The dance crowd had loosened up, thanks to a keg of beer behind a makeshift bar in the corner of a large open room. One or two couples swung across the dance floor. Another group made up mostly of men clumped around the keg of beer. Long metal tables beside the dance floor were filled with women gossiping about this and that.

"Where are the available men?" Cora Mae asked over the din, her head swiveling like a she-cat picking her night's prey. "I don't see a single one."

"Focus, Cora Mae," I said, watching her chest puff up in attack mode. "We aren't here for the men. We're working tonight."

"I'll see if I can find Tony," she said, stalking toward the male gathering.

"Look at that woman's walk," Kitty said, watching her. "I should take lessons."

"What's our plan?" I said, studying the crowd.

"We're winging it," she replied. "Let's spread out."

Sue, the credit union manager's wife, sat at one of the tables. She was as good a place to start as any. "Hi, Gertie," she said when I sat down next to her. Judging by the glassy cast to her eyes, she'd had a few beers already. "Heard you were in the credit union when that robber was killed."

I nodded. "How's Dave doing?"

"He's having a hard time of it. The acting sheriff is treating it like Dave masterminded the whole thing. Sheriff Snell is convinced he did it and has been following him around."

The beat of the music stepped up a notch. Cora Mae swung onto the dance floor with a man I'd never seen before and did some kind of tango thing in her spike heels. The entire room of people stopped what they were doing to watch her moves.

I had to practically shout to be heard. "I didn't notice Dickey around tonight. Someone on the roof killed the guy who robbed the credit union. I witnessed it. Why would Dickey be bothering Dave?"

I knew about the missing money, but wanted to hear her version.

"I'm surprised you don't know, what with the gossips in this town. Some money's missing and Dave can't account for it. They think he stole it."

"We all know that couldn't be true," I said to reassure her, even though he was the most likely candidate. I scanned Sue's outfit—worn stretch pants, scuffed shoes, and not a bit of jewelry other than her wedding ring. If Dave stole the money, he wasn't spending it on his wife.

Cora Mae's theatrics and a lively song drew out a group of women. Kitty danced by, her seldom-combed-out curls formed into bouncing ringlets that reminded me of miniature slinkys.

"You help out at the credit union, right?" I had to roar over the music that the DJ had cranked up several notches.

"Good thing I didn't work yesterday." She took a chug of beer, long and hard like she couldn't face their problems. "I wouldn't have been able to take it. You know, the guns and all."

"What do you do at the credit union? I never saw you behind the counter."

"I work in the office, doing whatever needs to be done. Why?"

"No reason," I said. "Want another beer?"

"Sure."

While I waited in the beer line, I thought about Dave and Sue. They'd had a shotgun wedding. Two teenagers having fun before realizing what work it could be. Three kids and fifteen years later, they were still together. Their dream, like every other parent's around here, was a good college education for their offspring. A hundred thousand dollars certainly would go a long way.

As the path ahead of me cleared, I saw Tony and Lyla serving beer from the tapped keg. "What can I get you, Gertie?" Tony smiled. Lyla made some kind of eye motion that told me to play it cool. Don't give her away.

"Two beers," I replied.

"We have to stop meeting like this," Tony said. "Or my wife is going to get suspicious."

Lyla's eyes narrowed. "Ohhh?" she said, making it the longest word I've ever heard. Later tonight I expected a phone call from the Trouble Busters' one and only client. She'd fire us if we continued to lose Tony, or kept tripping over him while trailing him. I was embarrassed, but tried not to let it show.

Tony laughed easy. "Just kidding, Lyla. Gertie was out in the woods this morning. The game warden had her treed. I see he let you go." Tony laughed again while he poured beer into a cup. "That Rolly sure takes his job serious."

"He's dangerous," I said, paying Lyla for the beers and picking them up. "See ya." At least I wouldn't have to worry about surveillance for awhile. My target was planted with the beer.

When I turned away, I noticed Angie Gates sitting at a table close to the keg. She was alone.

"Glad you're out of the hospital," I said. "How are you feeling?"

"Pretty good," she said, but she had her mind on something else. Angie checked her watch like the exact time mattered to her.

"Meeting someone?" I said.

"No. What makes you think that?"

I shrugged. "Guess I better deliver this beer before it warms up."

Angie had already glanced away. I moved past, then stopped to watch her. She seemed fidgety—nervous and wary. Maybe the blow to her head accounted for the edginess.

The seat where I'd left Sue was empty. I sat down, put the beers on the table, and took a sip from one. Where was Sue? Cora Mae had coaxed quite a crowd onto the dance floor, making it impossible to find anyone in the mass of humanity.

We were supposed to be interrogating suspects. Instead, Cora Mae was working everyone up to the point of collapse. How could she get any pertinent robber information out on the floor? While my eyes roamed the room without spotting my other Trouble Buster partner, someone sat down next to me. "I hope this seat isn't taken?" my man George said.

"Reserved for you." I grinned and passed the other beer to him. "I even have a cold beer ready."

"I like a woman who serves her man." George took off his cowboy hat with the snake curled around the brim and set it on the table.

"Let's not get carried away," I answered.

George looked great. He didn't have to wear oversized shirts to hide middle-aged flab, because he didn't have any. He keeps active by building things and tearing down other things, and he has a healthy interest in the world around him. While other men his age pound down six-packs of calories while watching sporting events on television, George maintains a scrappy, fit-and-trim physique.

I, on the other hand, could stand to lose a few pounds before my relationship with George went any farther than holding hands. I set down the beer as a first start toward better health. Fewer sugar doughnuts, less beer, more exercise, I reminded myself.

It's amazing what the possibility of romance can do to you. I'm self-conscious now in ways I never was before. George has been my friend for years, but until recently it never occurred to me to worry about my appearance.

"Want to go over to the church and see who's winning at bingo?" George asked. I translated that to mean he wanted to spend a few minutes alone with me. A warm thrill ran through my body, tingling my spine, making me feel flushed. Any kind of alone time wasn't easy to find ever since Grandma Johnson moved in.

We walked out to the edge of the parking lot where the lights didn't dilute the night stars quite as much. The air was cool and crisp. With George by my side and the sound of the dance behind me, I could have remained there all night.

I followed the stars of the Big Dipper from the top of the handle to the bottom of the dipper. I silently apologized to Barney for holding hands with another man. Two years had passed since he died. Part of me felt I was moving ahead too soon. The other part thought it was way past time.

George squeezed my hand like he knew my thoughts.

Barney didn't offer an answer to my dilemma.

Cora Mae popped out of a parked car, giggling and adjusting her clothing. She didn't see us, which was fine with me. I wanted to criticize her for playing instead of working, but wasn't I doing the exact same thing?

"I wish Cora Mae could find someone to make her happy," I said, after my friend and her mystery man walked away, clenched tightly together.

"She looks pretty happy right this minute."

We walked toward my truck, still holding hands. "What the ..." George stopped abruptly.

That's when I saw the dark form on the ground behind my truck.

And it wasn't moving.

EIGHT

PEOPLE DO STRANGE THINGS sometimes. The chance of me committing a weird, unexplainable act has risen exponentially with the passage of time. That means the older I get, the more likely it is that I will establish my own set of rules. For example, I really don't think I need a driver's license to get in my truck and tool around. Someday a cop will bust me and I'll pay the price, but the young whippersnapper police officer will let me off easy because of my age.

So why bother going to all the trouble of proving I can drive when I already know I can?

The reason I did what I did when George and I found the body was ... well, I can't explain it, because instinct took over. I wanted more than anything to sleep in my own bed tonight. So when I saw my Glock lying off to the side of the lifeless man, I knew what the term "smoking gun" meant. My fingerprints would be all over the weapon. Dickey would arrest me and throw away the key. I'd eat bread and gruel for the rest of my life.

So ... while George checked the man for a pulse, I pocketed the Glock. George bent close to the man's body. "He's dead," George said, confirming my fear. Now what? Once I stopped to think about disposing of a murder weapon after the fact, I realized that removing it from the crime scene isn't that easy.

I couldn't throw the gun in the woods. I was pretty sure even a ninny like Dickey would check the surrounding area. The garbage can wouldn't work either, for the same reason. I couldn't put it back in my truck for the same reason.

I could drive away in my truck and throw it into the Escanaba River, but that would entail moving the corpse. Also, I wasn't ready to give up my Glock. I just recently acquired it and had grown fond of it. The Glock was my security blanket.

"I'll go inside and call the sheriff," I offered, walking away quickly. "I'll be right back."

The band was taking a break, so the room noise had subsided. The keg was still the most popular spot to socialize. Kitty had commandeered a corner table with the nosiest, gossipiest bunch of women in the entire county. She noticed me right away when I rushed at her. Eye contact, a nod, and she stepped in right behind me.

"I have a gun in my pocket," I said, whispering in her ear inside the ladies room. "And there's a dead man outside."

"What do you need?" Not even a blink from her. I could have been talking about the weather for all the response I got. Someday I'd have to take the time to delve into her past. There's more there than meets the eye.

"The gun has to disappear before the cops arrive," I said, not quite believing that I was stealing the murder weapon and expecting my friend to help me. "It's mine and it's the murder weapon."

That got more of a reaction. Her facial expression didn't change, but her eyes widened.

"I didn't kill him. You can say no to getting involved," I said, hoping she wouldn't. "You're taking a risk."

"Hand it over." Kitty moved closer, opened her purse wide, and we made the transfer.

"Don't handle it without gloves," I said. "It's bad enough that my fingerprints are on it. I'm calling nine-one-one about the dead guy in a minute. Go now."

Kitty nodded.

I didn't have time to tell her the rest. That my Glock wasn't the only piece of evidence lying next to the dead man. There were two.

The smoking gun.

And the other?

A black Kromer exactly like the one worn by the credit union shooter.

———

"Someone's setting me up," I said to Cora Mae from the side of the gawking crowd of spectators. Word had spread fast. The music faded away and the beer keg wasn't the center of attention any longer. I saw Grandma Johnson working her way carefully down the church steps, which meant the bingo group knew, too. Sirens wailed in the distance. "My Glock was under the front seat of the truck," I whispered.

"Didn't you lock the truck's doors?"

"I thought I had."

Truth was, I never gave much thought to locking doors. It wasn't as much of a necessity as it was in a big city. Neighbors watched out for each other. We might be spread out, but our internal sensors go off at anything out of the ordinary. Try pulling over on one of our back roads and see how long it takes for someone to drive by and ask what you're doing. Two minutes tops. That's the most time you have.

Cora Mae couldn't rip her eyes away from the body. "Who would do that to you?" she asked.

"Same person who would do that to him." I pointed at the body.

Dickey, all puffed up like a rooster, strutted over, hitching his pants up and clearing his voice to get the squeaks out. He stared at the body like he didn't know what to do next. Our acting sheriff was getting more action than he knew what to do with.

"We're going to need to talk to everyone," Dickey hollered, losing a little of his college education. "All of you who were out in the lot any time during the evening. Come forward if that's you."

"We all came from the lot," a wiseacre from the back said. "How else could we park our vehicles and get inside."

"Very funny," Dickey said. "Let me rephrase that. Anyone who had any reason to be out in the lot other than to park their vehicles. There. You happy?"

I didn't have a choice, since George and I discovered the crime scene. I had to go up.

Cora Mae didn't move a muscle. We locked eyes. "What?" she said.

"Weren't you in the parking lot?"

"Yes, but …"

"You don't want the whole town to know you were making out in a parked car?" I finished for her.

She nodded.

"I guess we both have a secret to keep." I didn't have to mention how much bigger mine was than hers.

Everyone was mesmerized by the body. In Stonely, we don't often see something like this. But two in a row! First, the robber, who really was an awful robber. Now, this man.

He was the same guy who fired the killing shot from the roof yesterday. The shot that blasted through the window and pegged the robber in the head.

It was definitely him, I thought to myself, groaning inwardly when a state trooper pulled up right behind Dickey Snell's truck. That's all I needed, the state boys involved.

George walked over to talk to them, having helped take control of the situation prior to their late arrival. I hoped he hadn't seen me pocket the Glock. Not that George would tell, but too many people knew already. And I didn't want him thinking I was a crackpot, even though I was beginning to think I was.

The only way out of my murder weapon mess was to find the real killer before Dickey and the state troopers found me and the Glock.

Blaze pushed through the crowd. "What can I do to help?" he said, sounding sane for a change. My son had his ups and downs, but he also had brief moments of reality that were growing longer every day.

Dickey glanced at him with a lot of doubt in his eyes. "I don't know, Blaze."

"Where's the ambulance? Has anyone touched anything?" Blaze asked, assuming a take-charge position just like the old days.

Dickey relaxed a bit as Blaze spoke. He motioned to him. They stood over the body, talking low enough that I couldn't hear. Blaze walked up to the window of my truck and peered in without touching anything.

"Ma," he fired at me, after a moment of silent thought. "Why the hell are you at the center of everything that goes wrong around here?"

I had my boy back! Maybe not permanently. Tomorrow he might be fighting the war again, but for right now, Blaze was close to his old self.

"Gertie's nothing but trouble," Grandma said from behind me, clacking her new false teeth. She didn't notice me right in front of her. When I turned around, she jumped a foot. Pearl, next to her, clutched her heart.

Gossip is one thing. Grandma's disparaging remarks about the only family member who was foolish enough to take her in was another.

I made a suggestion to her through gritted teeth. "Go find Star," I said.

"And miss this! Fat chance."

I slid as far from the old-smelling woman as possible.

Between the excess law enforcement teams, they managed to separate out the potential witnesses. Grandma was forced into the nothing-but-gawkers group, complaining all the way. Star, who was supposed to be watching her, caught up and steered her toward the church parking lot.

The ambulance arrived and carted the body away, heading for Escanaba and the medical examiner's office.

Eventually George and I were the only bystanders still outside. We told our story, what little we knew—that we had wandered outside for fresh air and practically tripped over the body. That George had tried to find a pulse while I ran inside for help. Our explanation sounded honest and innocent. If only they knew.

"He had a Kromer," George said in case anyone missed it.

I had forgotten in the excitement. My attention had been more focused on the Glock lying in plain sight.

"That's the guy who killed the robber at the credit union," I said to Dickey. "I'm sure of it."

"You sure?"

"Positive."

"Hole in the front of his head," Blaze announced.

"Execution style," Dickey said. Like he'd know.

"Never saw the guy around here before the heist," I offered. "I think he was in it with the guy he killed."

"She's right," Blaze said, still right on track to a full mental recovery. However, the old Blaze never would have given me any credit. He would have escorted me away with a firm grip on my arm and told me to mind my own business. I liked the new Blaze better.

George stood close to me. "Two strangers, a bag of paper instead of money, and they're both dead with shots to the head." He shook his head in bewilderment. The snake wrapped around the brim of his cowboy hat seemed alive in the shadows.

"They had a partner," I said. "A third guy." It should have been obvious, but who knows with this bunch? The bad guys were picking each other off like dominos.

"Threesomes never work," Blaze said. "Two, sometimes, if they both keep their mouths shut. You put another guy in the mix, and it's always a disaster."

"Well," I said. "It isn't three anymore."

"Why'd it have to happen right behind your truck, Ma?"

"That's a good question, son."

My truck, my gun. Someone wanted me out of the way.

NINE

Word for the Day
Extirpate (EKS tuhr pay't) v.
Remove completely, exterminate.

Alternate Word
Higgledy-piggledy (HIG uhl dee' PIG uhl dee) adj.
Disorderly, jumbled, confused.

SATURDAY MORNING AT THE first crack of light, I bellied through thick brush, getting into position. Tony's bales of straw loomed ahead in the dark, like sinister wild animals. I wore my handy fishing vest crammed with supplies, including pepper spray, micro recorder, binoculars, and my stun gun. The vest made it even harder to snake along the cold ground.

Today, since it was the beginning of the weekend, the woods would be crawling with amateur turkey hunters, blasting at anything that moved. And here I was, dressed in camo, slinking through the brush. Why did I always get the worst surveillance times and the most awful situations? The Trouble Busters needed to come up with a more equitable plan for future events.

And the cold! I should be in bed with the covers pulled up over my head, with Fred snoring away on the floor. The house had been toasty warm when I left. Next time, I'd drop off Cora Mae and she could hang out on the forest floor.

I waited.

A while later when I couldn't feel my frozen feet anymore, Tony tromped in with a shotgun, set out a turkey decoy, and settled behind the straw piles. I heard a shot in the distance and a few turkey calls. Whether they were turkeys or hunters, I didn't know.

A roosting flock of turkeys could make a variety of sounds besides gobbles—yelps, clucks, and kee-kees. A lot of hunters don't know the first thing about their prey, which works in the turkey's favor.

Turkeys roost in trees. They like to travel with other turkeys. If the flock is scattered, they will regroup in the same spot within fifteen or thirty minutes.

This morning I didn't expect to see any. They might not be the smartest bird around, but they can outmaneuver a human. What does that tell you about our intelligence? Those birds were on vacation in parts unknown.

The sun rose higher in the sky, warming me up some. Once in a while, a shot went off. A squirrel jumped across the tops of the trees. A small DNR plane soared overhead, looking for illegal activities. I hunkered into the surrounding environment in my leafy garb and stifled a yawn. Thinking it must be afternoon by now, I checked my watch and found it was only nine o'clock. I laid my head on my arm and closed my eyes.

I must have dozed off, because when I raised my head there were voices coming from behind the straw pile. Tony wasn't talking to himself. He had company.

"Quiet down," Tony said, harshly. "Sound travels in the woods. Did anyone see you coming in?"

I heard mumbling after that, but couldn't make out the words. The only thing I was sure of was that the other voice belonged to a woman. At last! Action!

Their voices hummed across the windless and frosty morning like buzzing mosquitoes, but I couldn't make out any more of their words. I'd have to get closer. I dug my elbows into the forest floor and scooted forward, the micro recorder in my gloved fist. The woman's voice sounded angry, rising like flames.

"I don't believe you," she said.

"I'll take care of it. We'll be together soon."

"I've heard that before."

Tony's partner in his illicit affair was listening to the same old lies told to gullible women since the beginning of time. You'd think women would get a clue after generations of toilet paper promises.

Anger turned to soothing coos, soft giggling, and other sounds. I couldn't believe I was stuck in the woods in this position. I had some time to kill while they hanky-pankied, and I had a really full bladder. I scooted backward until the wild brush screened me from view. When I was sure it was safe to change positions, I did my business, took a sip of Tang from a small bottle, readjusted myself, and slunk back.

I was just in time to see the back end of the woman, retreating in the opposite direction. She had on woodsy colors and wore a cap that hid her hair. I wouldn't even be sure it was the woman if I hadn't heard her talking to Tony.

I quickly shuffled the binoculars from my hunting vest.

But it was too late.

I'd broken the first and most important rule of surveillance. No potty stops. That's exactly when the target will decide to move, according to my beginner's manual. And it had happened exactly that way.

I wanted to rush after her, throw caution to the wind, and collect on the Trouble Busters' manicures. But part of my job was to accomplish my mission quietly and discreetly, without alerting Tony. My professionalism kicked in and I held back.

I put adult diapers on my mental grocery list.

An hour later, Tony collected his decoy and whistled while he walked down the trail leading home.

The hours in the woods among the Jack pines and tamarack trees hadn't been a complete bust. I had the two lovers recorded on tape, and most importantly, I knew Tony was cheating on Lyla. It was a start.

———

"That dirty dog," Kitty said from my kitchen table. Fred slid his nose onto the table at the "dog" word and wagged his tail.

"I never would have guessed it," Cora Mae said, giving Fred a pat on the head.

We had polished off six freshly fried sugar doughnuts, two each. Kitty reached for a third. "We have the rest of the day off from following Tony," she said. "Lyla said he'd be puttering around the house."

"What if the woman in the woods was Lyla?" Cora Mae suggested.

I shook my head. "She knew I might be out there."

"Maybe she's a voyeur," Cora Mae said.

"A voyeur is someone who likes to watch sex acts," Kitty said. "The voyeurese would be Gertie, not Lyla."

"Believe me," I said, "I didn't enjoy it one bit. Besides, I know Lyla's voice. It wasn't her."

"Tony had his little breakfast love fest," Cora Mae said. "Good thing you were watching him, Gertie, or we would still be wondering about Lyla's accusations. I'm really disgusted with him."

"People aren't always what they seem," I said, knowing that true enough. I looked at Kitty. "Where did you hide the Glock?"

"Are you sure you want to know?"

"I'm sure. No one's going to hook me up to a lie detector while I'm still alive and kicking."

"It's all wrapped up in plastic and buried down inside my compost heap."

"Yuck," Cora Mae said. "That pile really stinks."

Composts are beds of rotten garbage that we use to fertilize our gardens. They need a perfect mix of carbon, nitrogen, oxygen, and water to decompose properly. We toss in all of our leftover kitchen scrap—except for meat and dairy, because those things attract vermin to the pile. We also add coffee grounds, horse manure, grass clippings. You name it. It goes in.

"You need to keep the proper balance of wet and dry," I said. "It smells bad because it's waterlogged. Right now, I'm glad it stinks, so no one will go near it. After this is over, you should add some paper and cardboard to soak up some of the water."

Grandma shuffled cautiously down the hall and plastered herself against the wall when she saw Fred at the table. "Get that thing outta my home," she said, forgetting who owned the house.

I flipped on the micro recorder to drown out my mother-in-law's crabs. Everyone listened to the few sentences I had captured on tape.

"Nothing but smut," Grandma said, edging warily around Fred and pouring a cup of coffee. "Who brought the doughnuts?"

"I did," Kitty said.

"Are they safe to eat?"

"'Course they are."

I snapped off the recorder since Grandma was determined to talk right over the voices.

Pearl, whose fifteen minutes of fame ended with the news of the second death, pulled into the driveway at about two miles an hour. I watched her do a jerky park between my truck and Kitty's rusted-out Lincoln.

"Pearl, get your hinder in here," Grandma called as Pearl walked in, wearing a little pillbox hat on her head. "We have a porno tape going."

"Goody," Pearl said, stepping it up a bit. Grandma set down a cup and saucer in front of her, sloshing most of the coffee into the saucer.

"What's the commotion?" Blaze said, rushing down the hall in his boxer shorts. He had his sheriff's hat on top of his head and an empty holster across his bare shoulder.

"We're holding 'em off," Grandma said, to get him going. "Where's your weapon?" She's the meanest woman I've ever known.

"Sit down," I told him. "We're eating doughnuts."

It's a good thing I have a big kitchen table. The six of us perched around the table like a bunch of monkeys. Once everyone had sugar fixes and coffee, I rewound the tape. We all listened again.

"That's Sylvester Stallone," Blaze said, piping up. "He's doing his Rocky character." It was going to be one of those days.

"You're right," I said to keep him happy. "Blaze won the first prize. Now, who is the woman?"

"Play it one more time," Pearl said. "I've heard that voice some-place before."

"Is it a porno star?" Grandma said. "Because if it is, I don't know any of them by name."

"You don't know any by sight either," Pearl said.

"She'd sit up and fly right if I caught one. I wonder where my gun went."

"It's someone from around here," Cora Mae offered. "She got a part playing the lead with Sylvester."

"I didn't hear anything about a movie star being in town." Grandma clacked her teeth.

"Shhh, everybody." I turned the volume up and replayed the tape.

"Not much to go on," Kitty said. "She said a total of eight words."

"They teaching you to count in that online class?" Grandma sneered. My friend and bodyguard had signed up for an online law degree class. Her goal was to get her state certificate to operate as a lawyer. The woman was book smart, no question about it.

But she didn't have a ready retort for Grandma. The old woman threw so many balls from left field, it was easier to ignore her than to participate.

"Where's my prize?" Blaze asked, looking around the room for a wrapped present.

"Have the last doughnut," Cora Mae said. "That's a good prize."

"That's one higgledy-piggledy tape," Kitty said, sliding her smug and competitive eyes over to me to catch my reaction.

"Got me again, Kitty," I conceded.

TEN

My agenda for the day was to interview the people involved in the credit union heist. Pearl didn't have anything new to add to her original sock-it-to-him story. I sent Kitty and Cora Mae to find Dickey in hopes they could pry information from him regarding the dead guy with the Kromer hat.

My two partners pulled out of the driveway with Cora Mae in the driver's seat. "Good luck," I called from the porch, hoping they survived.

Fred and I headed for the Trouble Buster truck, but we made it only halfway before being detected by the yard patrol. Guinea fowl flapped through the backyard like a carpet of locust, running as fast as they could on their scrawny legs. They circled Fred, pinning him in the center of the group and pecking his toes. He howled.

Last year, my first squawking flock consisted of six little guys, fluffy day-old keets with orange legs. They weren't all little "guys," since they've multiplied several times. They like to hide in tall grasses with their broods, depriving me of fried eggs. Instead, I get more of them to feed. It doesn't seem fair.

Guineas coined the term "free-range." Nothing can keep a guinea confined. They come and go as they please, roosting in trees or the barn, and they eat up weed seeds and bugs. Guineas like to dine on Japanese beetles and deer ticks. I've even seen one suck up a yellow jacket and go on hunting like nothing unusual happened.

They have their faults, though. With a machine-gun-like alarm call, they are the noisiest creatures on earth.

And they hate Fred.

He howled again while I waded in, swinging my arms and legs, parting a path to the truck where the enormous black coward was only too happy to hide. I had to leave the driveway at a rolling crawl to keep from running my guineas down.

Ruthie's Deer Horn Restaurant was on Highway M35, across from the railroad tracks. The train ground to a screeching halt as Fred and I stepped down from the truck.

"Hey, Otis," I called to the train conductor, who liked to stop at Ruthie's for coffee and tall tales. Otis Knutson's appearance meant Carl should be along shortly. Sure enough, Carl pulled in with George, and they watched me tie Fred to a post in the front of the restaurant where he could keep me in his sights.

My dog dislikes waiting in the truck by himself. When we're at Ruthie's, he settles for hanging around outside as long as I bring him a treat afterward.

The four of us took seats at the counter, lined up like a row of turkey targets. Ruthie swung out of the kitchen with a pot of coffee in her hand. She poured a round without being asked.

In the U.P. we take our coffee seriously.

The men ordered mounds of eggs and bacon and potatoes. I stuck with the coffee since all those doughnuts had sunk to the bottom of my stomach like lead weights. Spending a thoughtful moment covertly eyeing George's hunky body, I *had* to stop sucking doughnuts.

George winked. I smiled at him, feeling shy and self-conscious. Then we told Otis and Carl about the robbery and the dead guy at the dance. Carl, who lives about a mile from me, already knew most of it. Otis hung on every word. So did Ruthie.

When we finished, Otis leaned his tall, slim body forward and slapped the counter. "Holy Wah! What a story! Too bad Blaze is laid up. He'd get 'em."

I didn't mention that Blaze had been more interested in slinging his feet up on the desk than chasing criminals—that he chalked most everything up to kid pranks. And that was at his best, when his brain was at peak capacity.

Ruthie went into the kitchen and came out carrying three brimming plates. She set them down in front of the men.

"Where has Dickey been?" I asked.

Ruthie answered. "He has his nose to the ground like a bloodhound. He's accused every one of us by now. He had the nerve to suggest I might know more than I'm telling. Deputy Snell isn't welcome in my restaurant until he apologizes."

"Otis is right," Carl said. "We need Blaze back quick."

"Ruthie," I said. "When we were lying on the floor in the credit union, I saw the shooter on the roof. I'm sure the man George and I found behind my truck was the same guy."

"Was he wearing orange shoes?"

"What?" I had only been able to see the guy from his waist up.

"I saw someone on the roof, too," she said. "Well, part of him. Remember, I was ahead of you in line. When I went down on the floor, I could see the bottom half of someone walking on the roof." She wiped her hands on a kitchen towel and slung it over her shoulder. "He had on orange shoes just like the robber."

"Did you tell Dickey?" I asked.

"Sure I did. He wanted to check my closet to see if I had some. I tell you, I better not see him around my restaurant."

Orange shoes. This was the goofiest case!

George spoke up. "The guy behind Gertie's truck didn't have any shoes on at all."

"I'll be," I said. I hadn't noticed that small detail. Probably because I was so worried about the murder weapon belonging to me. I'd completely missed the dead guy's lack of footwear.

I had to get a break in this case soon. I didn't want to wait around for any more shoes to drop.

———

After feeding Fred a piece of George's bacon, I headed toward June Hopala's place over on Peter Road. June wasn't inside the credit union during the holdup, but she worked there part-time and I wanted to ask her some questions about Dave Nenonen, the manager, before I interrogated him.

At the moment, he was on my short list for criminal involvement. Money was missing from the vault, and Dave had the easiest access.

I'd run the scenario through my head enough times. I had a theory of my own, and it was holding water.

Somebody took the money before the robber even entered the building, took it days, maybe weeks or months before. That Somebody started getting worried. Eventually the money would be discovered missing, which the mastermind should have thought of in the first place. So Somebody planned a fake robbery. Kent Miller was supposed to escape with the pillowcase filled with play money. Everyone in town would think the thief had taken the hundred thousand dollars, when really Somebody had taken it.

Except the plan went south. Everything was working out fine until Dickey's deputy squad showed up. Then the rooftop shooter plugged poor Kent, and the hoax was up. Somebody must be really worried by now. The money was discovered missing and dead bodies were falling like meteor showers.

The real thief couldn't be Kent or the guy in the parking lot. They were pawns. The king, or queen, still was on the move. The little guys had been extirpated. How convenient was that?

Yes, Dave was on my suspect list, but I had a small problem with that. Why would Dave leave Angie behind the counter with her finger right next to the alarm button? If he stole the money, he'd want the robber to get away with the hoax. He would have made sure Angie didn't use her lethal finger. Yet she had. He hadn't tried to stop her.

And why would a stranger on the roof take out the robber instead of letting Dickey handle it? Unless he was afraid his frantic partner inside would finger him. Did Kromer man have the loot? Was he killed for it?

I hoped I'd have a clearer picture after talking to June.

Fred and I pulled into June's driveway. Fred started howling as I walked up to her neat and tidy little house—whitewashed with a cute picket fence and daffodils poking through the thawing ground.

I'd called ahead, so she was expecting me.

"Come on in," she called out with a warm welcome. "Have some taffy. I can't thank you enough for giving me your recipe. It's a family favorite. Hope you write your cookbook soon."

I wanted to say I'd have plenty of time from prison.

June seated me in her living room. That meant I was special company. A plate of taffy waited for me on the coffee table.

I peeled waxed paper from a piece and plopped the taffy in my mouth while June watched with a smile. I couldn't help humming, a family trait we had no control over. The hum happened when we sampled something really delicious.

June took a piece.

We chewed for a while.

"My daughter-in-law brought her kids over," June said after finishing her taffy. She rolled her tongue along the front of her teeth to dislodge the last sticky morsel. "They got a kick out of making it. They pulled and pulled."

"It's great family fun," I agreed.

I made taffy when the kids were growing up. We'd cook it to the right temperature, cool it slightly in long slabs, then grease our hands with butter and tag-team pull it. The first pull involved the entire taffy batch and two strong pullers, then later we broke it down into smaller strands so everyone could have their own. The longer we pulled, the creamier it got.

"When *are* you coming out with your cookbook?" she asked.

"My new business is keeping me too busy."

We took seconds and chewed some more.

It gave me time to study June. She was past retirement age, collecting her social security and working part-time at the credit union for extra pin money. Her husband died the year before my Barney passed on.

She had on a bib apron dotted with flowers and two pink foam rollers on top of her head. I'm a short woman, barely five-two, but June was even smaller and seemed to be shrinking as the years went by.

"You said you wanted to ask me about my job?" June said. "Are you helping Sheriff Snell with the investigation?"

"Yes, I am," I said. It was sort of true. "He needs all the help he can get." That part was absolutely true.

"I thought at some point he'd come by personally."

Meaning Dickey hadn't been here.

"What do you do at the credit union?"

"I open new accounts, although that part isn't very busy since pretty near everyone in Stonely and beyond already has an account. I also send out monthly statements and help Sue with the book-keeping part of the business."

"Dave's wife does the books?" This was important news that she had failed to mention at the dance.

"Just the basic stuff on the computer. She uses a program and plugs in numbers."

"It must be strange working with the manager's wife."

June shrugged. "I mind my own business."

What did that mean? I couldn't think of a polite way to ask for clarification so I just said it. "What do you mean," I blurted, "by 'I mind my own business'?"

June leaned forward. Her body language suggested busybody, exactly the opposite of her verbal comment.

Antithesis should be the word for today instead of … um … I couldn't remember. I hate when that happens. It was on the tip of my tongue, since I'd used it on the way over.

"Well," June said slowly. "If you asked me, I'd say Sue's been wearing some fine jewelry lately. And …" she dragged it out. "She and Dave are whispering about moving someplace warmer."

"We all talk about that every winter," I said for the sake of argument.

"Yes, but we talk about running down to Florida for a week or two in a mobile trailer. Dave and Sue are talking new condo development."

She threw me a meaningful glance to make sure I got it.

I did.

If they had the stolen money they might be biding their time, planning to live large later.

At June's insistence, I filled a vest pocket with taffy on the way out.

ELEVEN

TURKEYS HAVE BEEN AROUND for ten million years. They can fly as fast as fifty-five miles per hour and run flat out at twenty.

Michigan's DNR had a hard time re-introducing turkeys to the wild. After four failed attempts, they realized that a little illegal hunting was going on. Not always the bird-brains we like to think they are—the Department of Natural Resources fitted the birds with homing devices.

When Jim Johnson (not the same Johnson from Grandma's family tree) was busted at Ruthie's Deer Horn Restaurant with an illegal turkey in the back of his truck, the locals decided to back off and let the turkeys thrive and multiply.

The turkey I was gunning for was a bird of a different feather.

Fred and I were on our way home to check on Grandma and Blaze. I planned to heat up some pea soup I'd made a few days ago and make sure Star was keeping an eye on the home front.

About a mile from the house, I saw Blaze's family car traveling toward me. It zoomed by, but not before I got a good look. Blaze was behind the wheel and Grandma Johnson rode shotgun. She was short, but I could tell it was her because I recognized the hat.

I did a fast U-turn, spilling my unprepared German shepherd onto the floor. After several efforts at control, the Trouble Buster truck wound up in the ditch. By the time Fred crawled up and re-seated himself, and I backed out of the dip, there wasn't even a puff of exhaust smoke left to tell me where they were going.

When I walked into my house, the phone was ringing.

"I'm calling it off," Lyla said from the other end of the line. "Tony and I made up last night. It was all a big misunderstanding. I can't believe I didn't trust him. Please forget this ever happened, and don't tell anybody I hired you."

I hadn't seen this coming. The investigation was finally pro-ducing results. What a snake that guy was!

"Were you out in the woods this morning?" I asked, knowing the answer.

"No. That's a strange question. You know I do nails at the salon in Gladstone on Saturdays." Lyla sucked up a big breath and let it out. "You can still have the manicures for the time you put in."

Now what? Should I tell her about Tony's hunting expedition? How could I walk away, knowing what I knew? Did I have an obli-gation, a commitment to follow up?

Cora Mae would tell me to mind my own business, that I'd quickly become the bad guy if I told Lyla about Tony's woodland love nest. She would hate me forever for shattering her happiness, even if it was only a figment of her imagination.

I struggled with my conscience through a moment or two of silence.

"All right, Lyla," I said. "I hope it works out for you and Tony."

Yeah, right. Lyla had just purchased a time-share with another woman and didn't know it.

Next time I crossed that lying cheat's path, I'd zap him with my stun gun.

———

I checked the kitchen counter, but didn't find a note from Blaze explaining his absence from the house. Star answered her phone on the fifth ring, sounding like I woke her up.

"Grandma Johnson and Blaze are loose," I said. "What happened to you? You were supposed to watch them."

"I have an awful headache," Star said. That was her code word for a hangover. Sinuses are acting up again is how she explains it. "I talked to Blaze a little while ago. He went into Stonely for gas, then was going to drive Grandma to Gladstone for ice cream."

"Did it occur to you," I said, "that Blaze hasn't been cleared by the doctor to drive?"

"That's not what he told me."

"You can't believe anything he says. Did you believe him when he told you he was a five-star general? Or when he said the temperature at the hospital got so hot his watch melted off?"

Star managed to titter through her "sinus" headache. "I liked the blue diamond story best," she said. "We're all rich, if only we can find the gems."

The guineas alarm went off outside. When I glanced out the window, I saw Mary getting out of her car. "Oh, oh," I said into the phone. "Gotta go."

Mary looked rested and serene from her sabbatical away from Blaze. I was about to end that calm.

"Where's Blaze?" Mary said after greeting me. She craned her neck down the hall.

"He's resting," I lied.

"Everything go okay?"

"Perfect. He wasn't any trouble at all. He's almost normal again."

Mary started down the hall. "Thanks for giving me a break. I really needed it."

"Unless you want to end up right back where you left off all stressed out, I'd recommend heading home. Let Blaze sleep." My voice crept up a few octaves when she didn't stop. "Don't go in there."

"What's going on?" Suspicion crossed Mary's face. She opened the bedroom door. I thought about running for my truck and heading for Canada.

"Where is he?" she asked, keeping a level tone to her voice.

"I lost him."

"How long ago?"

"Not long. Rumor has it he's pointed toward Gladstone. He's with Grandma Johnson, so I'm sure he's all right."

We both thought about that for a minute. Then we scrambled for my truck. We moved so quickly Fred didn't know what was happening until we'd already squealed out onto the road, leaving him home alone.

———

Gladstone, Michigan is an easy twenty-minute drive from Stonely. It has a lot of amenities that are missing from our small town. For one thing, they have a main drag with cute business establishments—cafe, bookstore, coffee shop.

I turned onto Delta Street and angle parked in front of the Dairy Flo, Gladstone's premium ice cream shop. Ease of parking is another great thing about Gladstone. No parallel parking anywhere.

We jumped out and surrounded Blaze's car, which was parked right in front of the Dairy Flo. He rolled down the window with his free hand and took a lick from a vanilla cone. Grandma, I noticed, had a strawberry sundae.

"Hey, Sweetie," Blaze said to Mary. "What are you doing in Gladstone?"

"I just got home, Blaze. You aren't supposed to be driving yet. Remember what the doctor said?"

Blaze shrugged and took another lick.

"I've been watching him," Grandma said. "He's doing a good job. Why don't you two get yourself some ice cream and we'll have a little party."

My mother-in-law and my son looked just as normal as everybody else on this early April afternoon. The morning chill had disappeared, replaced by the warmth of the sun and a promise of spring peeking around the corner. We weren't the only ones at the Dairy Flo lapping treats.

"Okay," Mary said. "We'll have a little party together. And then Gertie will drive Grandma back home. I'll drive you home, dear."

"Gertie doesn't have a driver's license," Grandma said, tattling on me. "I wouldn't let her drive my lawn mower."

"Well," Mary said. "We'll figure something out."

While Mary and I waited in line, I kept a watchful eye on Blaze's car. Our turn came. While we were ordering, right there under our very noses, Blaze backed out of the parking space and tooled away.

Mary and I had to abandon our already ordered ice cream and race to the truck.

"They're headed for the lake," Mary said, not at all as peaceful as she was on her arrival at my house.

We drove past the Gladstone Motel and sped around the curve onto Lake Shore Drive. "I don't see them yet," I said.

We sailed past the yacht harbor and the lagoon. "There," I pointed. "By the Beach House."

"I don't know what it takes to ditch you two," Grandma crabbed when we forced them out of the car. I thought about slapping handcuffs on the old witch. "You sure can't take a hint. I want to spend time alone with my grandson."

Grandma's idea of quality time tended to highlight the wonders of discipline. Blaze's ears were lodged forward on his head more than they should be after all the ear twists he had to endure over the years. She'd still get a grip on them when he made her mad.

"I'm going to Kids' Kingdom," Blaze said, looking off to the right at a playground with an enormous wooden fort. To our left, tall grasses waved in the breeze and a walkway led down to the waters of Little Bay de Noc.

"I'll go with you," Mary said to her husband.

Blaze took off with Mary in tow. I heard him say, "Grandma said my money's hidden in the fort."

"You don't have any hidden money," Mary said. "You're still having delusions from the meningitis."

"Spoil sport," Grandma said under her breath. "Let's go look at the waves." She headed for the boardwalk.

The wind had picked up. White caps the size of freighters formed in the open water, rolled toward us, then broke and slammed against the fine white sand of the beach. My hair blew this way and that, covering my eyes until I held it away with a hand on my forehead. Grandma shuffled through the sand, then stopped. She cast a complaint my way, but the wind picked it up and carried it off in another direction.

A man and woman sat with their backs to us, wrapped in a blanket. Several other people walked along the beach. A dog loped near the water with no owner in sight.

My eyes latched onto two women with rolled-up jeans, wading out in the lake. One of them kicked her bare feet through the waves with angry thrusts.

April's air temperature, in spite of the wind, was fairly comfortable because of the sun's warmth. But stepping into Lake Michigan at this time of year had to be as cold as treading over ice cubes.

The great lake's water never quite warmed up enough for an enjoyable swim. I've been in it when the water was so cold my ankles ached from wading for only a few seconds. And that was in July!

I pulled the binoculars out of my fishing vest and focused in. The tall one had hair almost to her waist. The sun caught it just right, giving her head a halo effect. She said something before they turned around and headed for shore. She'd stepped in a little too deep because her jeans were wet. The other turned and I recognized her.

"I'll be right back," I said to Grandma. "I have to say hello to someone."

Angie Gates didn't see me approaching until I was almost beside her. When she did notice me, her eyes opened wide in surprise, and she backed up into the waves.

The credit union teller's face was blotchy, her eyes red from crying. Her hair whirled as the wind picked up, creating an effect right out of a horror flick.

I could see her mind working over the situation.

She took off running down the shoreline, pulling the other woman along, shouting at her to hurry. I knew better than to chase Angie. She was years younger and stronger than me, and whatever was happening to her to make her run away from me had given her added forward momentum.

The tall woman was beautiful, the kind that made me wish for one more go around in her body instead of mine. I never looked like that, even in my best year.

I glanced down at the waves near my feet.

Anyone who lives near the Great Lakes would know simple physics. Most things tossed into the waves would wash back up on shore. Unless the object filled with water and disappeared under the lake's sand carpet. Angie must have thought they would sink.

One did. I saw a flash of color before it vanished under the weight of water and sand. The other rolled toward me. With each new wave, it tumbled closer.

I kicked off my shoes, braced myself for the shock of cold water, waded in, and picked it up.

I held an orange sneaker in my hand.

TWELVE

"THERE'S A GANG UNDER the bridge," Kitty said from the front porch of her dilapidated house. Kitty's yard still looked like a junkyard, even after official town warning number three. But since she wanted to be a lawyer, I wasn't about to interfere. "They call themselves the Orange Gang."

Cora Mae guffawed. She had bobby pins stuck in her mouth while she wrapped Kitty's wet head in pin curls. One of them flew out when she laughed. "The Orange Gang, what a name," she said, talking out of the side of her mouth.

I sat down beside Kitty. It was the safest place to hide from the view up her house dress. I thought about the bridge Kitty had referred to, the Mackinac Bridge that connected the lower and upper peninsulas. "Tell me more."

"All we got from Dickey was a name," she said. "The dead guy behind your truck was Bob Goodyear."

"Goodyear? Spelled like the Goodyear blimp?" I scribbled in a notebook, listing names and drawing arrows between possible connections. All the lines looped and crossed until my effort looked like toddler scribbling.

Kitty nodded.

"Quit moving your head," Cora Mae complained. "Now I have to start that one over."

"I got most of my information from the Internet," Kitty said. "In the 1920s, the Purples ran the rackets in lower Michigan. They were tough. Tough enough to stand up to Capone and Scarface. Goodyear's gang comes from Grand Rapids and they're trying to emulate the Purples—graffiti, symbols, tough talk, and a color all their own. Orange."

"They probably picked orange because purple is its complementary color," Cora Mae said.

"Blue is," Kitty corrected her.

"Close enough," Cora Mae said, smashing a strand of curled hair against Kitty's head and anchoring it with two bobby pins.

"A gang," I said, in awe. In the U.P. we know about gangs. As in "let's take a picture of the whole gang in front of that wood pile." Or "Let's invite the whole gang over and polish off a case of Bud."

One time, a motorcycle gang stopped at Ruthie's on their way through Stonely. They scared a lot of residents that day, before moving on. Otis from the train is another gang member, the railroad gang.

But this was different. This was real, mean, and ugly, inside and out.

"Why did Bob Goodyear extirpate Kent Miller in the first place?" I wondered out loud, getting a kick out of my word for the day. "They both wore orange shoes, so they were on the same team."

Kitty shrugged, earning her a gentle slap on the top of the head from Cora Mae, the beautician.

I waited breathlessly for Kitty to use her word for the day again. I longed to watch her mouth form higgledy-piggledy.

"Just because they're in the same gang," she said, "doesn't necessarily mean they are best buddies. After all, they come from a lumpen society, which is probably rife with internal problems."

Lumpen? Rife? Where was higgledy-piggledy?

I didn't know what to say. Lumpen wasn't on my radar.

"They're riff-raff for sure," Cora Mae said through the bobby pins.

"Besides," Kitty said, "Dickey talked to Kent Miller's mother. His whole family lives in the Soo. The mother said he'd just started going down to Grand Rapids recently. She didn't know anything about orange shoes."

"That's a mother for you," Cora Mae said. She glanced at me. "What have you been up to?"

"Chasing my family across the county," I replied, giving them a short overview of my quest for the escapees. They laughed until tears ran down their faces. I guess you had to be there to appreciate the seriousness of the matter.

Then I got to the meat of the story. "Angie from the credit union was walking the Gladstone beach. When she saw us, she ran away."

"If Grandma Johnson was anywhere nearby, I can see why," Kitty said. "Don't take it personally."

"I'm not so sure," I said. "An orange sneaker washed up on shore."

"I'll be danged," Cora Mae said, while chewing a wad of gum. Her favorite exclamation is cripes, but recently she's added dang to her developing vocabulary. "Where's the shoe?"

"In my truck."

"We have to tell Dickey," Kitty said. I could hear the reluctance in her voice. Including the law in our operation was a last resort.

"I'm afraid you're right," I agreed, my feelings about involving the acting sheriff running along the same vein as Kitty's. "I'm going to heat up pea soup for the family, since we didn't have lunch. Unless you count the ice cream that I didn't get any of, thanks to Blaze. Then the three of us should go find Dickey and tell him about Angie."

"It wouldn't hurt to scope out her place first," Kitty said.

"After dark," I agreed, starting to feel night's chill in the late afternoon air.

"What about Tony?" Kitty asked. "Ouch, Cora Mae, watch those pins. You're digging into my scalp."

"Lyla fired us," I said, telling them about the phone call from Lyla and the cozy couple's re-alliance. "We're officially unemployed."

"You did the right thing by keeping quiet about the other woman," Cora Mae said. "You can't get involved in their marriage."

"Lyla hired us to get involved. I feel like I'm letting her down."

"I hope she's going to pay us for the work we did," Kitty said.

Now was as good a time as any to break it to my partners. "We had a trade agreement. She's giving us manicures." I slung it out there, and it hovered in midair.

After a second of dead silence, Kitty yelped. "What! I don't have any other job but this one! I was counting on cold cash in my hand." She stood up, hands on hips, and stomped a foot.

"Oh goody," Cora Mae said, holding one hand up for a quick assessment. "I want some of those acrylic nails, the French ones."

Kitty held her hands in my face so I could see her nails. I never noticed before, but they were chewed down into the quick worse than I remembered. "Do I look like a woman who cares about her nails? Do I? I have to pay for my online legal course. How am I going to do that?"

I'd never seen Kitty so mad before. She must really be desperate for money.

"We could have another rummage sale," I suggested, looking around Kitty's junkyard. "And Herb's bar needs a part-time bartender. Since my grandsons own it, I can get you in." I crossed my fingers and hoped that Red and Ed wouldn't mind that I was doing a little hiring for them.

"How soon?" Her voice was still angry.

"Anytime. Want to work tonight?"

"Saturday night will be too busy at the bar for a training lesson. All I know how to do is pour beer."

"That's great, because that's all anyone ever orders."

"Not tonight. We have a surveillance run. And you know how I like those."

———

Did Angie Gates kill Bob Goodyear behind the Trouble Buster truck with my Glock? Was she the third partner? Did she turn against the men, planning to keep all the money for herself? I thought about that while heating up the pea soup.

It smelled delicious, and I realized how hungry I was. Pea soup is a traditional Swedish dish that I learned to make from Grandma Johnson, with a few minor revisions. She used pig's feet or pig knuckles in hers. Mine is made with ham hocks. I gave the soup a final stir and processed some more information about Angie.

I'd seen her at the dance. She looked a little fidgety. I thought she was waiting for someone who was running late. The only thing I knew for a fact was she hadn't killed the robber because she'd been on the floor behind the counter klonked out. And I'd seen the whole thing happen. Did the orange shoes she was throwing in the water belong to Bob? Or was she a member of the same gang and hiding the evidence?

"It's ready," I called out to the Bobbsey Twins, who were napping in the living room. Blaze's large body covered the couch and Grandma slept upright in a side chair. Mary, who was watching the TV6 news had to shake them awake.

Fred ate with us, only his meal was in a dish on the floor. Kibble and a crumbled piece of his favorite—bacon.

"Pea soup's lots better made with pig's feet," Grandma said, before she even had the spoon to her mouth to taste it.

I sat down and ignored her while I ate.

Blaze hummed, carrying on our family tradition of humming when the grub was good. I smiled.

"Thanks for having us over," Mary said.

"You shouldn't have to come home from a trip and start cooking right away," I said.

Grandma humpfed. "You women don't know how good you have it."

"Sure we do," Mary answered, sweetly. That's Mary, always smoothing ruffled feathers.

"Don't patronize me," said Grandma.

"After we eat, I'm going out for a little while," I told them, confident that any trips they made would be on foot. Mary and I gave each other a conspiratorial glance. Mary had the keys tucked away in a safe place.

"Why don't you come over to our house?" Mary said to Grandma. "We can play cribbage."

Our family is a card-playing family. Anything we can deal out, we'll play. Rummy, Poker, whatever.

"Fifteen-two?" Grandma perked up. "Better than sitting around in this mess."

THIRTEEN

BEFORE WE DID ANY eye-spying or illegal breaking and entering, we wanted to make sure the acting sheriff wasn't slinking around near Angie's place. Dickey Snell's truck wasn't parked at the jail, so the three of us drove past his house in the Trouble Buster.

When Kitty had joined the team, she took over all remaining space inside the truck, so Fred had to ride in the back bed. He didn't seem to mind, sitting calmly watching the scenery go by. In the beginning I used to worry that he might jump out and get hurt. But he's a smart dog. It hasn't happened.

Almost every dog in the U.P. rides in the back of an American-made truck. Fords are popular here. One thing I never did though was put my kids back there. Some people even do that. You see them tooling down the road like they think it's a fun hay ride. Carrying kids in the cargo area of a truck is legal in Michigan as long as the vehicle is going less than five miles an hour. Can you believe those whacky laws?

The practice was a source of serious frustration for Blaze, who had to scrape more than one kid off the road over the years. Not to mention the parties of hunters, riding around in the back, drinking cheap beer, and falling out on their heads.

The lights were on at Dickey's house, so I drove past very slowly. "What do you see?" I said to Kitty, who was sitting on the side closest to the curb.

"I can see the top of a head," she said, rolling down the window and sitting as tall as she could. "That's Dickey's greasy comb-over turned toward the television set. Hit it. We're safe."

We turned away from the big lights of Stonely. The dark swallowed us up.

I'm not much of a night driver, especially in the twilight that comes right before true darkness. The residents of the U.P. don't believe in spending their taxes to promote light pollution, so we use our brights to watch for critters crossing the roads.

I had my partners helping me scout for possible problems when something went wrong with the Trouble Buster's electrical system. The lights stopped working as soon as we turned off US 41 and began to cruise toward Trenary.

I pulled over.

"Holy Cripes," Cora Mae said. "The world's gone black. Dang. What's wrong?"

"Lights are out," I said even though it should have been obvious to anyone with half a brain.

Kitty lurched out on her side, and we walked to the front of the truck and stared at the headlights. I kicked the bumper, hoping to jar something back in place. Kitty pounded on the glass.

Cora Mae, our resident electrical engineer, stepped out in her high heels and said, "The bulbs must be burnt out."

"All of them?" I said. "All the way around the truck?"

She nodded. "Do you have any spares?"

"Nobody carries spare light bulbs around. Besides, that's not the problem."

"We'll have to finish the mission in the dark," Kitty said. "It's not like we haven't done this before." Which was true. In the past, we'd evaded Blaze's wrath plenty of times by dousing the lights.

"Yes," I said. "But you were driving. I'm night blind."

And that's how race car Kitty got control of my vehicle. You'd think I'd learn from past mistakes.

We blew through Trenary like a renegade hurricane. Cora Mae had a grip on my lower arm so tight I thought her spiky fingernails might sever it from my body. Kitty yelled "yah hoo" when we turned left in the center of town and headed out past the cemetery.

I heard a siren. When I looked behind us I saw lights. None of the commotion was coming from my truck. "Cops," I said. "Now look what you've done! Nothing like calling attention to the fact that our equipment isn't working."

"I bet I can outrun him," Kitty said, but I was ready for her. I held the stun gun up and turned it on. The faint hum convinced her that I meant business. She pulled over. "I'm getting a ticket for sure," she said. "You should've let me outrun him."

"No way. And you're the only one in the truck with a valid driver's license," I observed. "Good thing you were driving."

The state trooper sat in his car for a while before he opened his door and slowly walked up to the Trouble Buster. That gave me plenty of time to stash my illegal weapon on the floor. Stun guns, I've been told, are frowned upon by Michigan's legal system.

Fred, former police tracking dog, recognized the uniform approaching. The traitor wagged his tail in either recognition of a fellow public servant or in gratitude for stopping Kitty and saving our lives.

"In a big hurry?" the trooper said to Kitty, who handed over her driver's license without being asked.

"I have a female problem," Kitty said. "I need to find a bathroom right this minute." Her voice went up a few octaves to let the cop know she was desperate.

"Stay where you are." He went back to his car with her license.

"That didn't work," Cora Mae said. "What next? Should I hit on him?"

"Let's see what he says first," I suggested.

The state trooper ambled back to the truck, unconcerned with Kitty's demanding bodily functions.

"Turn on the vehicle's lights," he ordered.

Kitty tried. Nothing.

"Thirty over." He scribbled something on a pad of paper. "Faulty equipment, unregistered license plate."

"This is my truck," I said to prove him wrong in at least one area. "And my late husband's license plates."

"The plates are registered to another vehicle."

"That would be the truck I rolled and totaled," I said to him.

"Plates have to be properly transferred." He ripped off a sheet of paper and handed it to Kitty. He gave me a paper that said I had to go in and prove the lights were fixed. Then he handed me one for the plate switching problem.

"This is outrageous," Kitty shouted after reading her ticket. "I'll see you in court."

"I'm going to follow behind you," he said, ignoring her outburst. "I want the vehicle parked until the faulty lights are repaired and the truck is properly licensed."

He sounded like Blaze.

I expected Kitty to turn the Trouble Buster around and head home. She surprised me. "What's Angie's address?" she asked.

I directed her along, making a left turn on the other side of Trenary, with our personal escort right behind us.

Kitty pulled into a short driveway leading to a cracker-box house and turned off the truck. The state trooper eased past us.

The lights were on inside Angie's house and all the shades were drawn.

We got out of the truck and waved to the cop when he made another pass.

With all the noise outside, I expected Angie to open the door and peek out. But she didn't.

"What should we do?" Cora Mae whispered.

"Knock on the door," Kitty said. She boldly marched up the two-step concrete porch and thumped.

Nothing.

Kitty tried the door. "Locked," she said.

Fred jumped down from the bed of the truck and followed me to the back door, where I rapped twice before realizing the door jamb had been pried loose.

"We're in," I whispered to my partners, pulling the sleeve of my hunting jacket down around my fist and opening the door through the cloth. "Don't touch anything." I cautiously walked in, listening for sounds, but an empty house has a certain feel to it and this one was empty. Angie and whoever had pried the back door lock were gone.

The teller wasn't a great housekeeper, but she didn't have much to work with. Every yellowed shade in the house was pulled down. Every light was blazing brightly. The kitchen sink was full of dirty dishes, the bed in the only bedroom was unmade, strands of hair coated the bathroom counter.

"Angie's moving out," Kitty said, eyeing up several cardboard boxes lined up along the bedroom wall.

"She was moving in," Cora Mae said. "That's what I heard. She's new to these parts. What do you think, Gertie? Was she coming or going?"

I scanned the interior of the tiny bedroom closet, seeing a line of metal hangers like the ones used by a dry cleaner. A few were thrown carelessly on the floor. Other than that, Angie's closet was as bare as Mother Hubbard's cupboard.

"Going," I said with confidence, "in a hurry."

"Or she would have turned off the lights," Kitty said.

What I didn't know for sure was whether or not her exit from her home had been voluntary. The jimmied door concerned me.

Angie Gates, I decided, was running with the wrong pack, a gang of Michigan predators. But whose side was she really on?

FOURTEEN

Word for the Day
Adipose (AD uh pohs') adj.
Containing animal fat: fatty.

Alternate Word
Pert-ner (purt nir) Yooper phrase.
An approximation: not exact

It snowed through the night, just a light dusting but enough for our needs. I could smell the rich aroma of cedar as George and I set out from the house to take our first sauna together. Dry stones gathered from the Escanaba River popped and hissed when George ladled on more water from a scoop in a bucket.

He had built the sauna behind my barn in his spare time with his own hands, cutting cedar planks to just the right lengths and pounding the boards together until the sauna stood tall and ready for social gatherings.

This crisp Sunday morning was as good a time as any to break it in with the man who made it happen.

George peeled off his jeans while I searched the ceiling, pretending to study the "stud" work. Cora Mae would enjoy the pun later when I filled her in.

I wore a pair of Barney's old sweatpants to cover my adipose thighs and a baggy T-shirt to hide my waistline bulge. When I sneaked a peek, George was pantless and in the process of unbuttoning his flannel shirt. The shirt was long enough to cover his fine buns, but not too long. I caught a glimpse of muscular, man-hairy legs.

What was I doing here watching George undress? What about my life-long commitment to Barney? My husband had visited me in my dreams last night, as he likes to do when I'm worrying about something. *Keep on living,* he'd whispered, *life is short, embrace it and squeeze out every happy moment you can.* I tried to get my arms around him, force him to stay with me, but he faded away in the early morning light.

"Are you sure you want to hold me to our agreement?" George said, grinning as he peeled off the shirt, exposing the rest of his body. I hoped if Barney was around, he couldn't hear my thoughts, because my lifelong partner never, ever looked like this.

"The agreement," George prodded, while my eyes wandered down to make sure he was holding up his end of the bargain.

I nodded, noting with relief that he wasn't in his birthday suit. "Swim suits," I sputtered. "That's the rule."

In the U.P. we like to take our saunas wearing nothing at all, except maybe a towel. That's the old way, and custom is important to us. This morning, I was throwing tradition to the wind and hanging on to caution.

Saunas are an important part of our community. They are healthy for us in mind and body. We sweat away impurities and increase our blood circulation without having to lift a finger. In fact, right this minute as George sat down beside me, my pulse went up a notch or two on its own.

"Well," he said, arching a brow and smiling at me. "Now it's your turn to get comfortable."

I was afraid of that.

What was it with males? Had they no modesty at all? I've yet to hear of one who wouldn't shed his clothes at the slightest suggestion.

"I'm feeling a little chilly," I hedged, as steam rose from the stones and raw heat slapped me in the face.

How could I show him my body? Barney was the only man who ever saw me unclothed. He got to start viewing when I was young, when my body parts were all where they were supposed to be. No varicose veins, no strange little warty things cropping up like weeds, no flab, no gravitational pull reworking my torso.

I couldn't even suck in my stomach any more.

And look at George! Other than a few wisps of gray at his temples, he had managed to maintain fighting trim. He hadn't carried three babies to term either, I reminded myself. And if he couldn't handle the sight of me, now was the time to find out.

I snuck another peek and saw him watching me with something new glimmering in his eyes.

"I won't look," he said, turning away.

"Promise?"

"Promise."

I wore a black one-piece bathing suit under my clothes, one with a flouncy little skirt that Cora Mae said would hide my flaws somewhat. The sweatpants landed in a heap at my feet along with my shoes and socks. I draped a towel around my middle and pulled my top over my head.

That's when I saw George staring. "You're a beautiful woman," he said softly.

I'm sure I blushed bright red, but the dry heat from the newly built sauna masked the embarrassment I was feeling. And I was feeling plenty.

By the time we ran out to roll in the tiny amount of snow on the ground, we were laughing like the old friends we were. And for a brief time, I forgot about Blaze's medical problems and Grandma's dementia and mean spirit. Temporarily I forgot about my widowhood and local murders and mayhem. I seized the moment.

————

Grandma Johnson had her chompers around a piece of Trenary toast when George and I came inside. Dickey sat next to her, bleeding cat hair all over my kitchen chair. I'm allergic to cat dander. Or maybe it was Dickey who caused my attacks.

"Make it quick," I said to him. "I'll start sneezing soon."

He knew that, because it happened every time he came too close in a confined area. You'd think he'd wear something other than that hair-attracting green suit when we had to deal with each other.

"You're allergic to that no-good, rabid dog of yours," Grandma said, dunking the toast in her coffee cup and glaring at Fred, who stayed calm through her tirade. He stretched out by the door, close to a fast route of escape. The only sign that he heard was a flick in his left ear.

I handed Grandma a piece of taffy. Her eyes lit up. That should keep her quiet.

"Let's hear what you have to report," Dickey said to me. "I spoke with Kitty this morning. She said to come see you."

I poured coffee refills for everyone and launched into my story about the Orange Gang and about running into Angie Gates at the Gladstone Beach.

"I'm a witness to that," Grandma said, stiffly around the taffy. "Don't forget."

"My mother-in-law saw Angie run away from me," I agreed. "That's when the orange sneaker washed up on shore."

"Are you alleging that the bank teller was involved in the robbery and homicides?" Dickey said.

Why was I bothering with Dickey Snell? He had plenty of book learning, but zero street-smarts. The proof is in the pudding, as Grandma says. Our acting detective was on the premises with his flock of turkey-brained assistants when the robber was killed. Murdered right in front of him and about twenty other locals. What does that tell you about Stonely's law enforcement officers' ability to protect its residents?

"Pretty obvious that she's part of it, don't you think?" I commented. "I should have had Fred along on the beach. He would have brought her back instead of letting her disappear."

Dickey's ears perked up along with Fred's. "What makes you think she's disappeared?"

"No reason." The last thing I wanted Dickey to know was that we had been inside Angie's house. "Just pondering out loud."

"Gertie and those two no-good friends of hers broke into a house last night," Grandma said, after spitting the ball of chewed-up taffy into the palm of her hand. "I heard them plotting on the telephone. Look at what I have to put up with! Living with criminals. And that dog!" She sucked the taffy back into her mouth.

"Why don't I help you to your room?" George said to her. "I can see you need a little rest."

I held my breath, hoping Dickey wouldn't pursue her accusation. A quick glance his way told me he wasn't paying attention. Grandma's crabbing can close off anybody's ears.

She grunted, but got up on her spindly legs and let George take her arm. "At least we have one kind heart around here," she said as they walked slowly down the hall. "Watch that animal when you come back down the hallway by yourself, George. He's vicious. Deputy Snell should take him away before he maims some little kid."

She stopped abruptly. I could see George trying to get her started again, but she shook him off and turned around. "I forgot something important."

"What's that?" I made the mistake of saying.

"I'm not talking to you. Sheriff Snell, listen up. I'm speaking to you, son."

Dickey blinked to attention.

Grandma shot a look my way. "You'll find something interest-ing," she said, "buried in fancy pants Kitty's compost heap. I'm pretty sure it's your murder weapon."

We stared at her.

"I'm not kidding," she said. "I heard them plotting away right here in my kitchen."

That was the last straw.

When I had more time, I planned to dig a hole in the backyard just the right size and plant a crab tree over the shriveled remains of one nasty old biddy.

FIFTEEN

DICKEY SCRUNCHED HIS NOSE and pulled away the worn piece of carpet Kitty had placed over the compost heap to help retain heat and speed up the compost process. No-Neck Sheedlo, his partner in crime, planted his wrestler-sized bulk right behind me and crossed his arms. When I looked back at him, he gave me a warning stare.

Go figure. Like they thought I was dangerous! The air was nippy, with the smell of possible rain or sleet. I zipped my old hunting jacket and pulled up the collar.

Grandma's pointed accusation of buried murder weapons had drawn out a curious group—the two local law enforcers, George, my traitorous mother-in-law, Kitty, me, and Fred, who ran back and forth behind No-Neck, aware that something was up and not liking it one bit.

"We need a pitchfork," Dickey said to Kitty.

"Don't have one," she lied as smooth as oil in a hot frying pan, which was pretty much where we were at the moment. "You'll have to use your hands."

"You do it," Dickey said to No-Neck, who shook his head violently.

"I'm pulling rank," Dickey insisted while rank, rotten egg odor assaulted our sensory glands.

"No dice," No-Neck said. "You can pull anything you want. I'm not doing it. Might be creatures living down there for all we know."

Dickey scanned our group.

"Don't look at me," George said. "You're the one who wants to wallow in muck."

"I told you," I said to Kitty after analyzing the murky mess. "You need something to sop up the water. It's out of balance."

Dickey threw the chunk of carpet down on the ground and rolled up his sleeves.

"Remember those compost worms you gave me for my birthday," Kitty said to me. "Wait till you see how big they got. Like snakes."

I stifled a chuckle at that. Worms turn food waste into rich soil. But you need a special kind. Night crawlers won't do it. They have to be red wiggler worms. None of them grow as big as a reptile.

But Dickey didn't know that. He hesitated.

"With a compost heap like this," Grandma said to Kitty, "you should be ashamed to call yourself a Yooper."

From the look on my friend's face, I knew she'd pitch right in and help me bury Grandma when I shared my idea with her. Kitty, though, might want to throw her in the hole alive.

Dickey dug in, making a face when his hand sunk into the mire. His arm went down and down until even his rolled-up sleeve sunk out of sight. Kitty had really buried the thing deep. When he hit pay dirt I could tell by the gloating expression on his face.

The rest of us looked on with disgust written all over us.

He pulled up a dripping, muddy bundle, managing to dip his knee in compost before he stood up.

I'd remained calm until now. The hunted look in my eyes must have warned George that I was about to attempt an escape through the backwoods, because he wrapped a comforting hand around mine and squeezed a reassurance.

In spite of all our denials of wrongdoing, Kitty and I ended up on the wrong side of the jailhouse bars, arguing about whose fault it was. We arrived at the obvious conclusion—it was the killer's fault and if we could weasel out of here, we'd hunt him down like the rabid skunk he was and haul him in, dead or alive.

George had gone off with Fred to figure out how to get us released, but his chances of success on a Sunday were slim to none. He also had the dubious pleasure of driving Grandma to her final destination.

"Don't take her back to my house," I'd raged right in front of her. "Give the battle axe to Mary and Blaze. She'll never step foot in my home again. Let her destroy their lives for a while."

Grandma boo-hooed into her embroidered hanky, but I didn't let her get to me. I had handcuffs on at the time and wasn't feeling overly generous.

"Obstructing justice at the very least," Dickey said, shaking his know-it-all weasel head from the other side of the jail bars. "Murder one at the most."

"You have no right to hold me," I said for the umpteenth time. "I had nothing to do with this."

"Me either," Kitty chimed.

Dickey turned to No-Neck. "Let's bring in Blaze and hear what he has to say. That was his firearm they buried."

While Dickey and No-Neck were gone, Kitty and I tried to escape through the ceiling tiles like we'd seen on television, but our efforts were wasted. In the movies the keys to the jail cell would be left dangling a distance away and a dog would bring them over. In our case, there wasn't a key in sight and Fred was with George anyway.

By the time Blaze walked into the jail with Dickey right behind him, we'd exhausted all means of escape, but had come up with a workable plan, as unsavory as it was.

We were going to give up an innocent man to protect the multitudes. My son had pulled fast ones on me more than once or twice, but I couldn't help feeling like a big smelly rat. Hopefully, the end would justify the means. I kept reminding myself that Blaze was used to jail bars from the other side. He most likely wouldn't mind sitting tight for a day or two.

Our idea was to convince Dickey that we had been covering for my son, that his mental illness had something to do with the parking lot murder.

As it was, Blaze helped out without even knowing about our covert plan to finger him.

"Ma!" he exclaimed when he saw me behind bars. He whirled on Dickey. "Release her right this minute. She didn't do anything wrong."

"The evidence says otherwise," Dickey said.

Blaze fixed him with a glare.

"Where's Mary?" I wanted to know, relieved that Blaze's wife wouldn't have to witness the shameful actions I planned next.

"Grandma Johnson showed up," Blaze said.

"The poor old lady is distraught," Dickey said. "She's been evicted from her own home. Mary's trying to calm her down. She has her hands full, so Deputy Sheedlo stayed to help her."

Kitty watched me closely for a signal and I understood that it was up to me; it was my family and she wasn't about to make the first move. What I wanted to do was give Dickey another sample of Blaze's mental state then … I couldn't think about it anymore, or I wouldn't be able to go through with it.

"Blaze," I said, with shifting eyes, so he knew I was talking around the others. "It's here." I pointed my head and eyes at Dickey. "Your fortune. He's had it all along."

"My money?" Blaze turned red.

"And your Glock." I put on the finishing touch.

"You have my weapon?" Blaze roared at Dickey, jabbing an angry finger at him. "I knew it was you, stealing my stuff. Give everything back. Where's my Glock?"

His eyes swung to the desk where the evidence bag lay. He had that faraway look he gets when he relives the war. Once he enters his own private universe, it's hard to call him back. Before I knew it, he lunged for Dickey's sidearm.

I hadn't seen that coming. I expected to implicate Blaze in the dead guy's murder and get either Kitty or myself released, so we could track the killer down as fast as possible and save the other two. Things weren't going as planned.

Blaze was fast for a big man. He had Dickey weaponless with his hands in the air in no time at all. "Throw me the keys," he hissed at him, never taking his cop-trained eyes off of Dickey. "Nice and slow. One-handed. Don't make me use this."

Before we knew it, the tables had turned. Dickey was behind bars, Blaze was searching for his millions, and Kitty and I had commandeered Dickey's sheriff's truck.

"Now what?" Kitty shouted from the shotgun seat. "We're in big trouble. We just broke out of jail and stole a law enforcement vehicle."

"We'll ditch the truck," I said, making things up as we went along. My investigation service was good training for what lay ahead. "Don't touch anything. We'll wipe it down and deny we ever took it."

"What will Dickey do to Blaze?"

"Let's stop at my house and pick up supplies," I punted. "Then we'll call Mary. She's good at negotiation, she'll figure it out. By the time she talks Blaze back from the war zone, we'll be good and gone."

"I was supposed to start my new job," Kitty said. "I can't believe it. We're in such big trouble."

She said the same thing at least six times before we pulled into my driveway, scattering guineas every which way. Then I spotted Fred, which gave me a brief moment of pure joy. George must have dropped him off before driving off to save us from the jail. I hated the thought of trying to explain the latest circumstance to George, so I didn't mind that he was gone.

Fred ran a cautionary loop around us, dodging hens, while I banged a hole in my barn with the front of Dickey's truck. Things weren't going as planned. Not at all.

SIXTEEN

BEING ON THE RUN isn't as romantic as I used to think. For starters, we had to figure out where to go—someplace not too far away so we could still work the case, but not too close so we would stay out of jail. Cora Mae's house was out as a place of refuge. So was almost everyone elses' that we knew. I couldn't involve my baby Star or Red or Ed, who were trying to scrape by at the bar.

I considered taking Grandma as a negotiating tool and threatening to dispose of her if Dickey didn't let Blaze go. But I'd rather drink Drano than spend three minutes with that evil woman.

I stuffed a suitcase with necessities in two seconds flat, then we raced by Kitty's house for her belongings.

No sign of trouble so far, no law vehicles in sight. Blaze must still be holding Dickey in lockup.

We ended up on Walter Laakso's rutty gravel road, kicking up dust with Fred riding between us. I dodged as many holes as possible but we still arrived a little rattled up inside.

Walter Laakso is suspicious of every single governmental body and totes a sawed-off shotgun filled with buckshot. That's why his place would be the perfect hideout. He's also nearsighted, so Kitty and I had to go through the standard ritual.

"Put 'em up," Walter said, leveling the shotgun our way.

"It's Gertie Johnson," I said through the open window, not getting out of the truck until introductions were over. "This is Kitty and my dog, Fred."

Walter lowered the weapon but I could tell he hadn't completely relaxed. I could also see that he hadn't done any serious grooming in awhile, and hadn't replaced his two front teeth since I'd seen him last.

"What you doing driving a sheriff's truck?" he wanted to know.

"Stole it," I answered truthfully.

He lowered the weapon. "Come on in then. I have a fresh pot of coffee ready."

Just like a Finn. They're always ready for company, even if it doesn't come visiting often. Walter's kitchen table wasn't exactly fit for guests—food grime cemented on it, cans of toxic yard chemicals scattered across it, unidentifiable spilled liquids.

Kitty didn't even notice. She sat right down and shoved a few items away before crossing her arms in the mess. I sat down gingerly beside her, avoiding any contact with the table.

"No brandy today," I warned Walter after he poured three cups of coffee and picked up a liquor bottle. He shrugged, splashed some in his coffee cup, and held up the bottle, offering it again with an expression on his face like we were missing out on something special if we refused.

"We need our wits about us today," I said firmly. "No brandy."

It's not our way to rush into the main topic without dancing around it for a certain amount of time. The weather is always good for a few minutes, so we did that. Then we had a few minutes of silence while we sipped our coffee.

"Gertie, you're purt-ner stressed out as a doe delivering a fawn," Walter finally said, using Kitty's word for the day. Come to think of it, I hadn't heard her use it even once. I guess we'd been too busy breaking laws to worry about a silly little word challenge.

"We're wanted by the law, Walter. We need help."

"Why didn't you say so right at the start?"

"I don't want to get you into trouble."

Walter snorted. "With that pipsqueak sheriff, Dickey Snell? I've buried lead around his feet more than once. He won't come out here without a death wish."

"I thought we might be able to hole up in your trailer out back."

"Help yourself. Stay as long as you want to."

"And we have to dispose of Dickey's truck and find new wheels. The Trouble Buster will stick out like a school bus."

"You two ladies settle in. I'll get rid of the truck and find transportation for you. Must be something drivable out in my yard."

Kitty laughed at that, finding a common connection with Walter. Both of them had junky yards filled with rusty old garbage. "For parts," Kitty would say when I asked her why she kept all that old stuff. You never know when you'll need a part.

Lugging our suitcases, we trudged around the back of the house to the trailer that Walter rented out to hunters during deer hunting season. Fred loped ahead, scouting for squirrels, thinking he was on vacation.

I put the key into the lock, heard it pop, and swung the door open. Kitty and I both gaped. Squirrels had been partying inside the trailer. We hauled the suitcases inside anyway, since we didn't have any other options.

I don't know how the rodents gained access, but squirrels had chewed on some of the electrical cords and had stored acorns and seeds in every nook and cranny. Mattress stuffing had been ripped apart as well as part of the insulation in the wall.

We set about putting things in order the best we could, then unpacked. I scooped dog food into a bowl from the tiny kitchen and fed Fred.

"We're going to need food supplies," Kitty said, looking hungrily at the bag of dog food I'd thought to bring with us. "We may be here awhile."

"I'm going to use Walter's phone to call Cora Mae," I said. Fred trotted along as I made my way back up the short trail.

Cora Mae answered on the first ring. "Mary's got everything under control," she said. "Blaze is in jail. They gave him some dollar bills and a pot of coffee and that made him happy. Tomorrow Dickey's having Blaze's Glock sent to ballistics, whatever that means."

Great. The killing shot would be traced right back to my son's weapon. At least, he'd be able to claim mental incompetence at his murder trial.

"Where are you?" Cora Mae wanted to know.

"In Walter Laakso's hunting trailer."

"Oh Gawd, I'd rather be dead."

"It's not so bad," I lied. We'd have to learn to make do from here on in. "We could use some food, for us and more for Fred."

"You better not go anywhere," Cora Mae said. "You and Kitty were just on the TV6 news and an alert keeps beeping and running across the bottom of the television screen. You should have thought about the consequences before you busted out of jail."

Well, that was true enough. "Adrenaline took over," I replied. "We couldn't stop ourselves."

"You're too impulsive for your own good," she said.

"Tell George we're okay and don't forget to bring food. Oh, and, bring your wigs."

"Why do you want my wigs?"

"We can't sit here doing nothing. We have a case to crack before Blaze ends up in prison."

———

At three o'clock we had a trailer-full of company. George and Cora Mae brought potato sausages, pasties, sugar doughnuts, and two wigs we'd used in the past for surveillance work. Kitty's was a black shoulder-length flip. Mine was long and blond. Cora Mae's favorite, a nifty red highlighted upsweep with a few dangly sexy curls, was already on her head.

Kitty's shifty cousin showed up, driving a purple sedan and making me more than a little nervous. The two of them went outside, Kitty in her new wig, and I could hear her negotiating with him over something. "I'll bail you out of jail next time. I promise," Kitty said. "I'm telling you, I need it right now."

A camera flash went off, and her cousin left.

I raised an eyebrow, but didn't want to question her in front of George and Cora Mae.

George went out to his truck and returned with four walkie-talkie handheld radios. After adjusting the frequencies to match on all of them, he distributed them, keeping one for himself.

Cell phone coverage in the Michigan U.P. is spotty at best. I've seen tourists standing on top of their cars trying to find signals. Most of us don't bother with them, preferring the old-fashioned land phones with cords.

"Don't use your radio unless you have to," George advised us. "Since anyone close by and on the same channel can hear the exchange, only use it in an emergency situation."

"What's the range?" I asked.

"Twelve miles," he answered, giving me a look like he'd seen more of me recently than the others suspected.

I tried not to blush. "That should be plenty of range as long as we stay close to Stonely."

We practiced testing, testing, one, two, three until we all had the hang of it. "I've got your purse in George's truck," Cora Mae said into her radio. That made me squeal with pleasure.

I can't live without my purse, and I don't mean that in the same way most women mean it. Mine is stuffed with all the equipment a good investigator needs. I ran to the truck and retrieved it. "All here," I said, rummaging through it. Handcuffs, whistle, mini recorder, and emergency money. I was set.

Walter came in just as we finished eating the sausages. "I got one of the vehicles running. Blue truck. I pulled it out next to the house. Here are the keys." He handed me two keys dangling from a key chain made from a loop of hanger wire. "And I took care of the sheriff's truck."

"Where did you leave it?" I asked, hoping Walter had moved it someplace where Dickey would stumble over it soon.

"Thunder Lake," he answered.

I stifled a screech. "Thunder Lake," I repeated. "Over by Cooks?"

Walter nodded. "Yup."

"Please tell me you didn't run Dickey's truck into the lake. Did you?"

"That's what you do, when you don't want it found," Walter said, looking at me like I didn't know the first thing about ditching a truck. "In the lake. On the deep end."

I was in so much trouble. All through Blaze's battle with meningitis, I'd wanted him to recover. I wanted my boy back just the way he'd been before he was struck down. Now, considering the latest development, I wished for the first time that he wouldn't recover anymore than he already had. It was a selfish wish. I knew that. But if Blaze got his job back and found out I was responsible for that truck on the bottom of the lake, there was no telling what he'd do to me.

That was, if Dickey didn't get to me first.

"I need a ride into Stonely," Kitty said to George while she adjusted her wig. "I'm working at Herb's bar tonight."

"You're not expecting to still go to work?" I was shocked. After all that had happened, she wanted to prance around town, risking detection. "Besides, I don't like the idea of involving Red and Ed."

"It'll be fine," Kitty said, waving away my concerns. "I'm going to work the bar for information. Once I explain to the boys how

I'm trying to help their uncle, they'll go along. And I'm not going to get caught."

"Our mugs were spread through the entire U.P. How are you going to manage that?"

"I'm posing as Kitty's sister. My cousin's getting me a fake ID. His forgeries are just as good as the real thing. Even if Dickey asks me for identification, he won't be able to tell the difference."

So that's what she was drumming up outside with her cousin. False identification. I wish I'd thought of that. "Can you get me one, too?"

"I had a hard enough time getting the one for me and I'm family. He usually charges a lot of money."

Cora Mae licked sugar off her fingers and chimed in. "Gertie, I'll fix you up so no one will recognize you." She dug in her purse and came up with a cosmetic bag. "Come over here."

I did what she said. When she was through with me I looked like a big city hooker with ... well ... never mind.

SEVENTEEN

THE PLAN WAS SIMPLE. George dropped Kitty at Herb's Bar after I made a call to warn my grandsons about Korky, the new blond addition to their staff. They must know their grandma wouldn't put them up to something like this unless it was really important, because they didn't ask any questions or complain about hiring a wanted woman impersonating someone else. Kitty, I mean Korky, would keep her ears open, stir up conversation, and see what rose to the top.

Fred would stay with Walter, since the beast was the most recognizable member of the outlaws. An enormous black German shepherd with red, devil eyes would be hard to miss coming at you. Fred seemed to like Walter and especially appreciated the wealth of snacks on Walter's kitchen floor.

Cora Mae and I decided to do some surveillance work over at Dave and Sue Nenonen's house. Since he was the credit union manager and Sue worked for him, doing the books, they were at the top of the suspect list. And if June was right, Sue had been talking about condos and had been seen wearing expensive jewelry.

Along with counting on gut feelings, an investigator has to know a lot about human behavior, has to zero in on anything out of the ordinary. Any little nuance (one of last week's words for the day) can be important. Dave and Sue had my full attention at the moment.

We stood next to an old blue truck in Walter's driveway. It was the rustiest thing I'd ever seen in my life. When I opened the driver's door, it creaked and resisted, and I thought it might fall off soon. The bench seat was shredded, probably by the same squirrels that trashed the trailer, and even the floor boards were rusted away.

"Don't start in on me," I warned Cora Mae, who was scrunching up her mouth to give me grief. "We have to make do with what we're given." She slid in without a single word, but her face said it all.

The truck started right up. When we left Walter's house behind, we could see the road through the holes in the floor.

Dave and Sue had a big house compared to many of Stonely's homes. That meant they had two living rooms and a dining room. Most of us had kitchen/dining combinations. All-in-one. And their separate family room moved them up to the upper-crust level. They even had a two-car, attached garage. Dave was an important citizen with a responsible position, and I always thought he worked hard for his money, so I wasn't as offended by his display of wealth as some were.

I knew all about the interior of their home from my part-time seasonal job as census taker. What a dangerous job! Almost more hazardous than the investigation business. I'd been chased by vicious dogs, had doors slammed in my face, and even faced a few shotguns and threats to my life. I wasn't sure I'd continue in the position when census time came around again.

"Mortgage must be pretty high," I said, while we watched the house from the truck.

"Now what?" Cora Mae wanted to know. "This isn't going to get us anywhere. What are we waiting for, sitting in this smelly, dirty old truck? Something died in here and I don't want to know what. I suppose you think someone with orange shoes will come out of Dave and Sue's house and we'll walk right up and make a citizen's arrest?"

I felt like I was with Grandma Johnson.

"The census badge won't work," I said, thinking out loud. "It has my name on it."

Cora Mae's eyes widened like platters. "You aren't going up to the door, are you? That would be crazy." Then she started laughing, easing up a little. "But look at you! Nobody would recognize Gertie Johnson under all that makeup." She peeled off her black rain jacket, jiggled around in the seat until she had it out from underneath her and handed it over. "The hunting jacket is a dead giveaway. Put mine on."

Cora Mae is taller than I am, so when I stood up outside of the truck, the coat came down to my ankles, making me feel very private eyeish. Blond hair, black raincoat, a pair of Blublocker sunglasses to complete the disguise. The only thing missing was still in my purse. My friend watched me palm the sheriff's badge I'd purchased from Blaze's law enforcement catalog. She shook her head.

Brash, bold, full of bravado. That was me. I felt like Lana Turner or Lauren Bacall. Not quite as tall, or thin, or young. But an investigator has to do what an investigator has to do. I would walk into their house and meet them eye to eye, without a clue as to a plan of action. What else was new?

"I'm with the Soo police," I said to Sue, trying for a husky voice to go along with the new me. "I'd like to ask you a few questions about the robbery and murders."

"My husband isn't home," she said, squinting at the badge as I waved it quickly past her.

"You're the one I need to talk to."

"You can't come in without a warrant. I saw that on television. And I'm certainly not inviting you in. I don't even have to talk to you without a lawyer present. And …" Sue stared at my face. My heart did a flip. Had she recognized me? "… you have a glob of lipstick on the corner of your mouth. Right here." She brushed a finger across her own lip to show me where it was. Of course, I slid my fingers along the wrong side. "The other side."

"Thanks."

"Come back when you have a warrant."

I'd watched enough cop shows to know what to say next. "You can cooperate or we can take a ride downtown." I was thankful Walter's truck was parked behind a big spruce tree. Only the front bumper showed through the dense pine needles.

"Why is Sault Ste. Marie involved?"

"Kent Miller was from the Soo. I caught the case." I tried on a little cop lingo for size. It fit well.

"What do you need to know?"

"We're curious about your sudden financial windfall. We have witnesses saying you're wearing fancy jewels and talking about buying a condo." At the moment, Sue didn't have anything valuable hanging from her neck or wrist just like at the dance. Her only piece of jewelry was a wedding ring with a modest diamond.

"Dave and I went through all this with the local sheriff."

"Go through it again for me."

Sue leaned against a porch rail and wrapped her hands around her arms against the chilling evening. I hadn't noticed before, but night was settling in quickly. "My father died down in South Carolina," she said. "He lived in a trailer with no air conditioning. He ate breakfast on Saturday mornings at banks when they gave out free pastry and he handwashed his own car. I didn't think he had a nickel to his name until a lawyer called. My father left me a million dollars."

"Holy shmo…" I almost forgot myself in the excitement.

"That's what I said at the time." Sue gave me a sad little grin. "I'd rather have my dad back than all the money in the world. Please don't let this get around the community. We're keeping it to ourselves. You know how people are?"

"Flashing jewelry around town isn't the way to keep that secret."

"That was my mother's necklace. I only wore it to church. But I hear what you're saying. It's cold out here. I'm going in. You can find out the rest from Sheriff Snell."

When I got back to the car, Cora Mae was on the radio with Kitty. "Get down to Herb's right now," Kitty said. "Angie Gates is sitting at the bar."

I put the pedal to the metal and almost rammed my foot through what was left of the floorboard.

———

Kitty met us in the parking lot.

"Are you sure?" I said, stepping out of the truck and noting four other trucks in the gravel lot. "You never met her. How do you know?"

"I saw pictures when we went through her house." Kitty's black wig bounced as she spoke. "But look in the window and *you* tell *me*."

We slunk over to the window. "That's her," I said.

"Now what?" Cora Mae said. Just once, I wish that woman had an idea of her own. My mind was ready to explode from having to make all the decisions.

"How'd she get here?" I asked. "Is she with someone?"

"She came in alone."

I walked along the back of the trucks in the parking lot, recognizing every one of them. Looking in the window again, I saw four locals huddled together at the bar. Angie sat off by herself, nursing a beer.

"She was asking about you," Kitty said, saving the best for last.

"You're kidding. Last time I saw her, she ran the other way."

"She wanted to know where to find you."

"What did you tell her?"

"I didn't. But I carded her."

"And?" Kitty was going to make me drag it out of her. I was tired and had lost my patience. I wanted to handcuff her to the back of Walter's rust bucket and drag her down Stonely's main street.

"Her real name is Shirley Hess."

"Send her out."

"Well," Cora Mae said. "Now we're getting somewhere."

Just in case it was a setup, Cora Mae and I hid around the back of the bar until we were sure Angie was alone. She walked out and wandered along the parking lot scanning the shadows.

I could hear country music playing inside. Angie looked lost— young and afraid.

When we stepped out, she saw us right away and started hurrying away.

I realized she might not recognize me with the blond-bombshell hair and black trench coat. "It's me," I called. "Gertie Johnson."

Angie hesitated then turned and approached cautiously.

"Where's your car?" I asked.

"I ditched it and hitched a ride from a gas station in Gladstone." She came toward us. Cora Mae had pepper spray in her hand, ready for action at the slightest wrong move. My stun gun was two fingers away. "I need your help," she said.

"In case you haven't been watching the news, I have troubles of my own."

"You're an investigator. I want to hire you."

"I'm listening."

"Private, please." She eyed my red-bunned partner.

Cora Mae, never too interested in our company's business end anyway, went into the bar to hang with Kitty. Angie and I sat in Walter's truck. My minirecorder was on.

"I don't know the guy who tried to rob the credit union," she said. "I don't know the other guy either. I want to get that straight right away."

I nodded to encourage her.

"I saw you pull one of the shoes out of the water," she said. "But you have to believe me."

"Why do you care what I think? What does it matter? I'm persona non grata with the local law."

"Like I said, I need your help. Those shoes I threw in the water had been planted in my house, in the basement. Someone's trying to implicate me in the robbery, or the murder behind your truck, or something. And I'm scared."

Angie or Shirley really did look frightened. "What's your real name?"

"Angie."

"Why the fake ID?"

"Like I said. I'm running scared. Fake IDs are a dime a dozen. I've had them since I turned sixteen. Used to get into bars long before I was legal. Whoever's after me won't be looking for Shirley."

"Why would someone be looking for you?"

"I pushed the emergency button that brought the cops, remember?"

"So someone wants revenge?"

"I guess. I was packing up some of my things last night when I heard a noise at the back door like someone was breaking in. I went out a window and ran away as fast as I could."

"Where are you staying now?"

"I won't tell you. But it's someplace safe."

"Okay. Let me get this straight." I watched a local stagger from the bar. Angie and I scooted down a little in our seats and waited for him to drive off. "You want me to find out who is setting you up?"

"No," she said, watching my face for a reaction. "I know who it is. But I need you to prove it."

EIGHTEEN

Word for the Day
Credulity (kruh DOO' luh tee) n.
A tendency to believe too readily, especially with little or no proof.

THE ONLY CONSTANT IN my life early Monday morning was my dog and my word for the day, which I had made up ahead of time and found in my pant's pocket. I'd lost my home, my family, and my new significant other, who I had advised to stay away from me. All lost because of one impulsive, foolish escape act. I should have stayed where I was and talked my way out of jail instead of running like a coward.

Looking around my dilapidated hideout, I couldn't see what had attracted me to this kind of life. The romance had gone out of the idea as soon as I found myself homeless.

I have to stop impulsively seizing moments.

But I still had my word—credulity.

Angie Gates was hiding something, but for the life of me, I couldn't figure out what it was. After my partners and I had left Herb's bar, I'd driven down the road and parked. Sure enough, a car pulled into the bar's parking lot ten minutes later and Angie had driven off in the passenger seat of a small dark sedan.

So much for her story of leaving her car at a gas station and hitchhiking to Stonely. One lie. How many others had she told me?

Today I intended to find out.

Kitty, lying next to me in the double bed, woke up slowly, groaning, and stretching. I flung off the covers, let Fred outside, and started coffee in the miniature-sized kitchen. The coffee gurgled and filled the trailer with wonderful aroma while I dressed in sweatpants, T-shirt, sweatshirt, and sneakers.

Last night we had tailed Angie and the driver to a house in Gladstone. Today we would stake out her hiding place and renew our investigation of Tony Lento.

I poured two cups of coffee, let Fred back in to eat his breakfast, and nudged Kitty awake. "Get up," I said. "You can sleep later."

"Tony Lento," she said after sitting down at the table. "Angie's accusing one of Stonely's most prominent citizens of grand theft. We better reserve judgment until we have some proof."

"I caught him cheating on Lyla. That's not very upstanding."

"Depends on what's standing up," Kitty said, chuckling.

I sipped coffee, feeling my body respond to the warmth of the liquid gold and its caffeine blast. Angie Gates had dropped a bombshell on me last night. Tony Lento, she said, was in the perfect position to steal from the credit union.

"How so?" I'd asked.

"He's the accountant."

Well, of course, I knew Tony was an accountant, since that was the main reason we had to follow him far and wide all over Tamarack County. He usually handled small businesses. His accounts were spread out. But I hadn't tipped to his connection with the credit union.

Sue did the bookkeeping, Angie explained, Tony took the financial information forward from there. The teller claimed she knew for a fact he was the thief. He knew she knew and was trying to implicate her, maybe even kill her.

Whether her story was true or not, both Angie and Tony could do with some surveillance. Since Lyla had fired the Trouble Busters, we no longer could get information from her on Tony's whereabouts.

Kitty yawned, stretched some more, and took big swigs from her coffee cup. "If Angie's so worried about her health, why doesn't she take off out of the U.P.?"

"She called into work and told them she had a death in her family. She's off for the week until she decides what to do. She kept talking about quitting but she hasn't done it yet."

"What rotten luck. She just moves in and blam, she's in the middle of a robbery."

I thought the same thing.

"How much is she paying us?" Kitty wanted to know, giving me one of those it-better-not-be-in-manicures looks.

"Two hundred dollars." I didn't mention that Angie couldn't produce a down payment.

"That's not much dough."

"No, but we have the same goals. We're trying to break the case for Blaze's sake anyway. Wish I could visit him."

"Maybe we can. Dickey isn't at the jail every minute."

One of the radios lying on the table sputtered and blew static. George's voice came through and we chatted about last night and what our plans were for the day, using a slapped-together code.

"Toodles asked me to drive her around," George said. "And help find Tigger."

I bet she did. Cora Mae, aka Toodles on the radio, might be my best friend, but when it came to men I didn't trust her as far as the barn. And she'd had her sights on George for the longest time, only backing off when I made it very clear that he wasn't available. Cora Mae isn't known as the Black Widow for nothing.

Tigger was code for Tony, like Tony the Tiger.

"I don't think that's such a good idea," I said, ignoring the fact that I'd told George just yesterday to stay away from me while I was a fugitive. "I'll go with you. Toodles and Big Ma can ride together."

"Best to keep you j-walkers in the same vehicle," George reasoned, rightly. J-walkers being our code for jail breakers. "If you split up, you'll be twice as likely to be spotted."

"Not to mention that whoever we're with will be in hot water."

"That, too."

"Thanks for helping, Sweet Cheeks," I said. "I know I've been a lot of trouble."

"You're worth every bit of it, Muffin Cakes."

Kitty rolled her eyes to the heavens, reminding me that our conversation wasn't exactly private.

"Let's get dolled up and hit the road," I suggested to her after reluctantly signing off.

"One more cup of coffee," Kitty whined. "I'm still sleepy."

A shotgun blast finished waking us up. Kitty and I stared at each other. "Walter has company," I whispered, running to a trailer window that faced the house. I lifted a corner of an old sheet Walter used for drapes and stuck an eyeball out.

The visitors were focused on Walter's trigger-happy welcome, so I took the opportunity to raise the window a bit. Kitty inched up behind me.

Dickey and No-Neck were sitting in a gray minivan with the windows rolled down. Dickey stuck his greasy, combed-over head out. "Put that weapon away," he shouted at Walter. "Why do we have to go through this every time?"

Walter fired another shot into the air. "I told you before and I meant it. Get off my property."

"I should incarcerate you, Walter. You can't take potshots at the sheriff."

Walter cocked his sawed-off shotgun and beaded in. "Come and get me, why don't ya, ya candy ass."

Dickey sat back and closed his eyes. I could tell he was wondering what to do next. When he opened them, his head swiveled toward the trailer. I didn't have time to duck, so I froze where I was.

It works with deer. They need scent and motion before they spook. If you stand inside, without moving a muscle, they can be looking right at you and not really see that you're there. But turkeys can see you right through the glass even if you don't breathe. Hopefully my deer tactic would work with the acting sheriff.

Finally, Dickey turned his attention back to Walter. "I'm assuming you are a man of your word, so I'll settle for a few answers," Dickey said. Walter didn't blink. "I'm looking for two jail breakers and a missing sheriff's truck. You haven't happened to see either of those three items, have you?"

Walter lowered the shotgun and grinned through empty front gums. "If I did see your blame truck, I'd pitch it in the lake."

"You have a serious problem with authority figures, Walter."

"Only the live ones."

Walter stood firm, his feet spread apart, the shotgun cradled in his arms like a baby, while Dickey reversed gears and pulled out backward.

"Well, Muffin Cakes," Kitty said to me. "We have work to do."

I lowered the corner of the sheet and plopped blond curly locks on my head. "After you, Big Ma."

NINETEEN

A PRIVATE INVESTIGATOR IS like a chameleon. We have to blend with our environment, morph with whatever colors we're up against, catch the wind and ride it.

So when Angie's partner-in-crime left her house on Dakota Street in Gladstone and drove over to a fitness center seven miles away in Escanaba, there wasn't any question in my mind. I was going in after her. Kitty dropped me at the door and roared off to watch the house in case Angie decided to move while her hostess was gone.

If Blaze had been functioning on all cylinders and still in his position as sheriff, I would have asked him to run the car's plates last night. Calling Dickie was certainly out of the question for obvious reasons. If I wanted to know her name, I'd have to introduce myself.

"Laura DeLand," she said, accepting my offered hand when I burst in behind her. Laura DeLand had the face of an angel. She should have been modeling in New York or making movies in Hollywood instead of hanging around the sticks.

"I'm thinking about joining the club," I said. "Will you show me around?"

"That's *my* job," a pip-squeak at the desk said.

"I'll do it," Laura offered, smiling through perfect teeth. "Come on."

The fitness room was packed with every conceivable type of health nut fanatic. This morning, without realizing it, I had donned the perfect clothes for working out in a gym. I noticed, though, that I was dressed more like the men than the women. Laura and the other females wore spandex—clingy, flexing material that showed off every hill and valley. I'd rather dive off the Escanaba River dam head first onto concrete than expose that much of my body to total strangers.

I could see the outline of Laura's belly button peeking out below tight fabric. Every guy in the place had his eyes on her. She didn't seem to notice.

We hit the treadmill. Mine had more bells and whistles than a rocket ship. Laura set me up on a level course and showed me how to slow it down and speed it up. A television screen in front of us was showing the Upper Peninsula morning news.

Mug shots of Kitty and me flashed on, and the anchor said something I couldn't hear over the machines and chatter. Where in the world did they get such bad photographs? Kitty looked like a post office wanted poster. Instead of sixty-six, I could have been twenty years older than my real age. Dickey had used a picture of me before I changed my hair color to red. One more reason not to change it back.

I wished I had added a little more eye liner and lip liner like Cora Mae had shown me. Someone used a remote to increase the sound. A cute TV6 newscaster was warning all of the upper peninsula that two women were wanted for questioning in a Stonely death. A suspect was behind bars. The escapees might be armed and dangerous.

Grandma Johnson must be swallowing her uppers over this. She never missed the news. It gave her something more to crab about. I could just hear her.

Some wiseacre next to us said, "They sure look deadly, don't they?"

Someone else tittered. "That big one could do some damage."

"The little one looks like Aunt Em."

"Those are the most dangerous ones."

"Hey," Laura said to me. "I think I saw that woman on the beach in Gladstone."

I pulled my blond curls over my face and strode along on the treadmill at an easy pace. "No kidding," I answered.

"Really. I was walking with a friend when that woman tried to approach us. My friend started running, saying let's have a race like the old days. But she looked frightened." Laura's forehead crinkled in thought.

"So," I said, eager to redirect her. "Are you new around here?"

Laura DeLand was one of those people who shared easily. Within a few minutes I knew that she had graduated last spring from DePaul University in Chicago and had landed a job as a reporter with the Escanaba *Daily Press*.

I slunk a little more under my hair when I heard that. Geez. A reporter! Why couldn't she work at the paper mill or the Dairy Flo. Just my luck.

I increased the machine's pace by pressing a button and walked faster, thinking hard. Maybe this whole situation could be turned to my advantage.

As an investigator I had to take what came my way and put a spin on it, just like a newspaper reporter might do when she's writing a piece for the paper. "I have a story," I told her. "If you answer a few questions, I'll give you something to get you a big raise."

Laura looked interested.

"Meet me outside when you're through," I said, getting off the machine by letting go of the rail and sliding off the back end. It wasn't the most graceful landing I've ever made.

TWENTY

I KNEW HOW LONG it took a young woman to finish a workout and gussy herself up, because I went through it when I raised Heather and Star. I had to wait through Laura's shower, blow drying of really long, thick hair, and a fresh makeup application from a tote bag full of supplies. After checking on her progress several times, I hung around outside with a cup of coffee from the café next door.

"Big Ma," I said into my radio while sitting on a street bench. "What's happening over your way?"

No response.

"Big Ma, calling, Big Ma." Maybe the information about the radio had been exaggerated. The range was supposed to be twelve miles. Kitty was seven away. I was ready to give up on raising her when I heard her voice.

"Hunh?" she said. Not exactly the fancy vocabulary of a woman taking an online legal course.

"Were you sleeping?" I asked. "You were. I can't believe it."

Kitty snapped to and denied it, but I could hear the confusion in her voice that heavy sleep brings when a person is startled awake.

"Where's you-know-who?" I asked, realizing we had forgotten to give Angie a code name. Kitty better know the answer. Here I was risking bone-breakage and ripped muscles while she sawed lumber.

"Our target's standing still," she stuttered a few seconds later, like it was fresh news to her too.

I signed off and waited some more.

Finally, Laura appeared and we agreed to slide into a booth at the café, just like in the movies. Laura had paper, pen, and a recording unit that she set in the middle of the table.

"No taping," I said, then remembered my own little unit. I secretly rifled through the purse on my lap, found it and turned it on.

"You said you had a story," Laura began.

"I do, but no taping. And I ask my questions first."

"Okay."

"You protect your sources, right?" I'd watched enough crime shows on television to know the drill, but she was young and might not understand all her professional ethical duties.

"I won't reveal your identity, if that's the way you want it."

"Ready for your first question?"

"All right." A waitress brought coffee for Laura and gave me a refill.

"Tell me about Angie Gates."

"Who?"

"Angie Gates."

"I've never heard of her."

As it turned out, Angie Gates wasn't really Angie Gates. Another lie from the credit union teller. Her real name was Shirley Hess. Laura had met her in college. Shirley left school after her freshman year. They kept in touch and Laura had offered Shirley a temporary place to stay. Shirley had decided a few days ago to make the move to Lower Michigan. She had been at Laura's house since yesterday, finalizing plans.

She had told me she was taking the week off to decide what to do next. What about the teller job? Had she given her employer any notice?

"When's she moving?" I wanted to know.

"She's still packing up her things and she's waiting for a delivery. A week at most, she thought. Why are you asking questions about my friend?"

"I can't tell you that, and you'll be better off if you don't mention our conversation to her. What kind of delivery is she expecting?"

"Some items she bought on eBay. She doesn't have an address yet where she's going, so she had them shipped to my house."

"Has she ever mentioned someone named Tony Lento?"

"Not that I recall."

My purse started speaking.

Toodles to Muffin Cakes I heard coming from inside it. The mini recorder flew to the floor when I fumbled with the purse. *Sweet Cheeks and I are on to Tigger.*

I turned the radio off as Laura retrieved my recorder from under her seat. She took a long look at it. "You recorded our conversation without my permission?" she said, a little anger in her voice. "At least

140

I was aboveboard with my intentions." She opened the unit and removed the tape. "If you want this back, you have to let me record your story."

Who knew someone as young as Laura could be so tough and street smart? I had to give her credit, she had me cold. Now I had to decide how important the tape was. Then I remembered that my conversation with Angie in the bar's parking lot was on it. And the female voice in the woods where Tony had his secret little love nest.

"Deal," I said, reaching out and turning on her recorder. "Let me start at the very beginning. You better get a refill on your coffee. We'll be here a while."

I had to take off the wig to convince her that I was Gertie Johnson, the one who had every cop in the U.P. searching for her. Laura stared at me with big, round, eager eyes. To a cub reporter, I must be a gift from heaven. I told her almost everything, even information that had been kept out of the newspapers. I told her about the robbery and the pillowcase filled with paper, about money missing from the credit union, about the dead guy and the Orange Gang. I even told her about Blaze's Glock and how Kitty and I ended up in jail because we stole the weapon and buried it in a compost heap.

What I didn't want her to know was the extent of her house guest's involvement, how Angie, or Shirley, or whatever her real name was had made several accusations against a local resident, how she wanted me to prove that he had set her up to take the fall for murder and bank robbery. I didn't want Laura to know how Shirley had hired me and lied to me. The more I thought about it, the more I was convinced that the alarm button-happy teller might be somehow involved, in spite of her denial.

Was Shirley Hess sending me on a wild goose chase? Was she talking turkey or crying wolf?

I couldn't put it together. She had saved the credit union from a robbery, or so she must have thought at the time, until the pillowcase was opened. The robber had even clunked her with his gun. And it was obvious that she didn't have thousands of dollars of stolen money, because she couldn't come up with a single dollar for a retainer for my services. And she was frightened enough to hide in Gladstone and plan an escape.

Another contributing factor was the dead guy's missing shoes. Someone had taken them off his feet, and that someone could have been Tony Lento. I'd seen him at the dance. He had the opportunity, money was the motive.

But why would anybody plan a heist and risk life and freedom to steal wads of paper money?

I watched Laura trot to her car, hauling her reporter equipment. "Can I get a picture of you?" she asked, straightening up from the backseat with a camera in her hand and a big Cheshire cat grin on her face.

We found a spot behind the fitness center where I could remove my disguise and brush out my hair. I cheesed for her several times before I saw a picture on the back screen of her digital camera that I liked well enough to want printed in the Escanaba newspaper.

What they've done with cameras since my day is truly amazing.

Before she left, she gave me her business card.

TWENTY-ONE

To SAY I WAS jealous and distrustful of Cora Mae would be a huge understatement. George Jack Erikson was going to get an earful from me, that was for sure. So was my best buddy, the man stalker.

Either she learned to drive alone pronto or she stayed home. No more teaming up with my man. It felt good to say that. My man. Barney had been my one and only until he drowned. It took me a long time to get past that, and I wasn't going to blow it. And Cora Mae was going to keep her mitts to herself.

I felt bad about my feelings, but not bad enough to change them. Cora Mae had gone through every single man in the U.P. except the one she was out joy-riding with.

I couldn't help but be suspicious.

"Toodles, where are you?" I said into my radio. "Big Ma and I are near the big city. And remember that other ears could be on our frequency."

Toodles purred back, "Sweet Cheeks is talking to me. Wait a sec."

I regretted giving George that moniker. At the time it was great fun, but it sounded pornographic coming out of Cora Mae's mouth.

"I'm back," Cora Mae announced. "Stay where you are. Tigger's heading your way."

"We're trading places as soon as possible," I said into the radio. "We'll wait in the pines near the cemetery and stay with you until Tigger reaches his destination. Then you and Big Ma can team up, maybe get that manicure you've been talking about."

"Roger and out, Muffy."

———

They came up around the bend into Escanaba so fast I had to run a red light to stay with them. Tony blew through the intersection with a speck of yellow showing on the traffic light overhead. George made it on full yellow and I squealed out trying to tuck the butt-end of Walter's rust bucket in under the changing light. I didn't make it. Solid red.

I checked my rearview mirror for cops. The coast was clear. Luck was on my side.

"He's heading toward the hospital," I guessed, turning onto Ludington at the next light.

At first I thought Tony must be visiting a patient, or maybe he did financial work for the hospital. But when he turned into a lane that ran around the back of the building, I spotted a hearse next to an unmarked door. Tony pulled into a small parking lot. George had no choice but to continue on.

I got a good look at the hearse. It looked like every other death mobile I'd ever seen. "That entrance leads to the morgue," I said.

By the time we circled back around, Tony was standing by the door with a heavyset woman and a young guy wearing orange shoes.

I almost panicked until I remembered our disguises. We passed within three feet of Tony without drawing any attention from him. By the time we found parking spaces, the three of them had disappeared inside.

"Now what?" Cora Mae said out George's passenger window. She looked way too comfy to me.

I yanked her door open and rearranged my envy-green face into a smile. "You and Kitty are through for the day. She's going to give you a final driving lesson on the way back to Stonely."

Cora Mae looked at Walter's truck. "Not in that old thing?"

"A driver needs to know how to handle all kinds of vehicles. Up and out."

We changed places and I watched Cora Mae jerk out of the parking lot, riding the brake all the way.

"I don't know how you women roped me into this," George said. "I'm losing a day's work while I consort with criminals." He had a grin on his face, so I knew he didn't really mind. "I kind of like you as a blond."

As much as I wanted to stay with George and listen to his sweet talk, I had a mission to accomplish. Tony Lento was in the morgue with one of the members of the Orange Gang. "I'll be right back," I said, before slinking over to the entrance door and scouting for trouble. Then I heaved my shoulders back, raised my chin, and walked down an empty hall that smelled of disinfectant and something worse. Hushed voices ahead slowed me down. I slid to the side of the hall and pretended to look for something in my purse.

"I'll give you fifty bucks," Tony was saying, "if you give me a name."

"Don't got no name, Man." I imagined those words came from the Orange member. It had to be him. He sounded hostile. "We pickin' up one of our own. Leave us be."

"A hundred. I'll give you a hundred bucks."

"You want I should shoot you right here in the morgue. Then you won't have far to go to get youzself pumped up with preservatives. Save on the cost of the amblance."

"God, jeez," Tony said, sounding shocked. "Put that thing away. I'm going."

I began walking slowly back the way I came. Tony breezed by me like a hound dog fleeing from a skunk. He glanced sharply at me, decided I wasn't a threat, and kept going.

What was the name he had been hoping for? Did he want to find out who the leader of the gang was? But in the movies, gang leaders liked everyone to know who they were. They didn't hide behind other member's skirts. Or in this case, behind their shoes.

If Tony was trying to finger Shirley, like she said, why was he creeping around the hospital trying to collect information?

Tony? Angie? Shirley? We had some serious credulity going on here. I was pretty sure I'd used my word for the day incorrectly, but no one heard, since it was just a head thought.

After Tony drove away, George and I waited in the hospital parking lot while a casket was loaded into the back of the hearse.

Then we walked over. I flashed my law badge. "Undercover," I muttered.

"We ain't talking to you," Hostile Boy said.

"I'm sorry for your loss," I said to the heavyset woman. She nodded.

George strolled over to talk to the hearse driver. His job was to find out which one of the gang members was in the coffin. Kent Miller from the Soo? Or Bob Goodyear from Detroit? I had a pretty good idea, judging by the speech patterns coming from the angry one.

Dialects are another thing a good private investor should be able to distinguish between. When George held up two fingers I knew I was right. Bob Goodyear. The shoe-less dead guy George and I had found behind my truck. The one wearing the Kromer who had picked off his own partner.

"Were Kent Miller and Bob good friends?" I asked, directing my question at the woman who must be Bob's mother.

"I told your people already. I never heard of that other guy."

"He wasn't no real Orange," Orange Shoe said.

"He was wearing your colors when he went down," I said, re-arranging a loose blond curl and readjusting the Blublocker sunglasses hiding my eyes.

"He was nobody and nothing. You have to concentrate your efforts on things that count. We wants to know who did Bobby." He shoved a stiff finger into my shoulder and brought his face close to mine. I smelled fear and I was pretty sure it was mine. "We take care of our own. We be back."

"Your guy killed Kent Miller. I saw him fire." I could see the pores in his face. The hate.

"That was Bobby's business. Not mine or yours. Bobby was set up. Come on, Ma, let's get outta this place."

Ma! I caught the connection between the dead man, the hostile Orange gang member, and the heavyset woman. "I didn't get your name," I said.

But Bobby's brother had turned his back on me.

TWENTY-TWO

"This is the Detroit bank calling," I said into Walter's phone. "Which one? Uh...Detroit Savings and Loan. I need to talk to Dave Nenonen. I'll hold."

Walter leaned against the kitchen sink drinking a latte—half bottom-dregs coffee, half brandy. Five o'clock on Monday afternoon must be the start of happy hour at the Laakso household. Kitty had gone back to the hunting trailer to put pasties in the oven. Cora Mae was studying Walter's dirty kitchen table for creepy crawlers.

"Mr. Nenonen," I said when Dave came on the line. "I'm calling about Angie Gates. She has applied for a position with our bank. Can you give her a good reference? Um...that's right. You didn't know she was leaving? Well, this is awkward. Yes. Thank you."

I hung up. Dave thought she was coming back to work on Thursday. As I suspected, she was slipping out of town without a goodbye party.

"Aren't we supposed to be working for Shirley?" Cora Mae said. "Instead we're tailing her and verifying the truthfulness of every word she utters." Cora Mae studied her new manicure, the French thing with white tips. "Lyla does a nice job with nails," she said. "And she's got troubles at home again."

"Happy ever after didn't last too long," I commented.

"Lyla thinks Tony found out that she put us up to watching him."

"Impossible," I said, sheepishly remembering when the local warden had outed me in the woods right near Tony's turkey blind.

"She thinks he was being nice to her just so she would call off the dogs."

"Is that what she said? Dogs?"

Cora Mae nodded.

I glanced down at Fred, who was lying at my feet, licking a paw. I decided to take that as a compliment. We could have been called much worse.

"Are we rehired?" I asked. That would be a bonus. We were trailing him anyway. Two paychecks for one job. One from Lyla, one from Shirley. I'd like that. We'd have the best fingernails in Stonely and have the money to pay for matching pedicures. I sighed at that thought.

"No," Cora Mae answered. "She says she doesn't want to know what he's up to. She's fed up and thinking of leaving him."

Serves the dallying fool right. Poor Lyla, though. Realizing you're married to a cheating spouse has to be tough.

Walter had finished his second latte when he said, "Think I'll go down to Herb's Bar for a while."

Cora Mae, Fred, and I went to the trailer and sat down to steaming pasties. Fred had one too.

"While Cora Mae had her nails done," Kitty said, splashing ketchup on her pasty and handing the bottle to me. "I talked to Star."

My baby girl. I had forgotten her in all the excitement. She must be worried sick about me.

"She says hi and will you hurry up and solve this case so she can quit babysitting Grandma Johnson."

So much for family loyalty and concern. "I hope you didn't tell her where we were," I said. "She'd probably turn us in. I'm thinking Star might have more of her grandmother's genes than she should."

"'Course I didn't tell her. Star's been to the jail to visit Blaze. So far he's happy locked up. He's bossing Snell around, trying to run the show. Blaze told Star a few things he overheard about the murders."

"Like we can believe anything Blaze says," Cora Mae added, truthfully. My son hadn't been a natural born liar before the brain disease struck.

"It depends," I said, ready to defend Blaze. I can say anything I want about him, good, bad, or terrible, but that doesn't apply to other people, even friends. "You can judge by what comes out of his mouth. If he's a five-star general in search of blue diamonds, or if he's showing you his new dog and you can't see the dog because it's invisible, that's made up."

"In other words," Kitty said. "If it's far-fetched, don't believe him."

"Right," I agreed. "So what did he hear?"

Kitty added more ketchup to her pasty. "The Detroit guy on the roof was wearing Onni Maki's Kromer."

"I thought the hat was strange considering that he came from Detroit," I said. A troll doesn't usually wear a Yooper hat. I had rolled the stolen hat idea around inside my head earlier.

"He took it out of Onni's car."

Cora Mae made a face when she heard the name. Onni Maki is seventy years old. He wears gold chains around his neck, a pinky ring, and wraps his hair over a big bald spot. He's also a widower and thinks he's the hottest thing in the U.P. He was one of the first men in the county that Cora Mae had rejected after one date. Onni had made Cora Mae pay her own way. "Pond scum," she said under her breath.

Kitty scraped her plate and looked around for more pasties. She knew there weren't any left. It was just wishful thinking. "Onni was part of the posse outside the credit union. Bob Goodyear was trying to disguise himself with the hat."

"Instead it made him stand out."

"Blaze said Dickey's been tracking the Orange Gang. I guess they're a tough bunch. But none of them knows the first guy, the robber. Bob Goodyear must have hired Kent Miller to go in. Dickey thinks he shot him because the robbery went wrong and he was worried about being identified."

"That's the only reasonable part of the whole thing," I said. "Bob and Kent decide to rob the credit union. Kent goes in, wearing orange shoes. He steals a pillowcase filled with paper. Angie who is really Shirley sounds the alarm. Bob kills Kent to conceal his identity. Then someone kills Bob just for grins. And, oh yes, the credit union has been robbed, but at a different time than the robbery, and the money is still missing."

"Right," Kitty said.

"But," Cora Mae asked, "wasn't it dumb to wear orange shoes? They led right to the Detroit gang."

"Not to mention the stupidity of stealing paper," I said. "Kent couldn't have known he had a fistful of paper. He had to have thought he had money. And the orange shoes haven't helped any of us solve the case. So maybe the shoes were a blind lead, meant to confuse us."

"Well it worked," Kitty said. "I'm confused. We have to straighten this out so we can quit hiding in this sorry excuse for a home."

Cora Mae was thinking hard. "What if Bob set up Kent? He sent him in knowing he wouldn't make it out alive. He and someone on the inside had already taken the money."

"That won't work," I reasoned. "If Bob took the money, he wouldn't want Kent to get caught holding paper. That would lead to a full investigation, which it did, and then everyone would know the money was missing, which they did."

The more I thought about it, the more confusing it became. "All we have to do," I said, letting Fred out of the trailer to do his business, "is find out why Kent stole play money, find out why Bob killed him, figure out who killed Bob, and find the missing money."

None of us said anything for a while. We were out of ideas. The orange shoe business had preoccupied us for too long. During the robbery, I remembered thinking the robber was insane to wear orange shoes in a holdup, especially if they led somewhere. Maybe it was a ruse, after all.

Maybe we should concentrate on our own backyard a little more. That left Shirley, Tony, Dave, and Sue. All were insiders and had the opportunity to steal from their employer.

I scraped my plate and started a sink of hot sudsy water.

That's when someone opened up on the trailer with an automatic weapon.

By the time I whirled around and realized what was happening, Kitty had blown off the chair she was sitting on. She hit the floor seconds before Cora Mae and I took a similar dive. Only ours was voluntary action, Kitty's had external force behind it.

"I've been hit," Kitty screamed, clutching her chest and rolling onto her side.

Frankly, I was relieved to hear her speaking, even if I hated what she said. Blood seeped through the fingers clutching her chest. She looked down. Her hands weren't staunching the flow.

"I never expected to go out like this," she moaned. "I always thought it would be my heart that gave out, with the extra pounds and all."

"Shush," Cora Mae said. "You aren't dead yet."

Up until now, Cora Mae has been the one with all the questions and insecurities. What are we going to do next? How are we going to handle this mess? Why do we have to drive around in this cruddy vehicle? Why? Why? Why?

I'd never seen her react under real pressure. I was witnessing it now.

"Nine-one-one," she screamed into her radio, louder than she needed to. I assumed for our attacker's benefit. I threw the kitchen table on its side and scooted between it and the refrigerator, dragging Kitty with me the best I could, considering she outweighed me by at least a hundred pounds. Her legs were still exposed, but there wasn't anything I could do about that. Cora Mae was behind the wood-burning stove with her back up against the wall dividing the living room and bedroom. She continued to shout our emergency into her radio.

Where was Fred? At first, I thought he was inside with us, but then I remembered letting him out. Please Fred, be off chasing squirrels on the opposite side of Walter's house.

Too bad Walter was down at Herb's Bar or he would have taken care of the madman with his arsenal of stashed weapons. If only I could get to the house and find them. But I didn't have a chance.

Another volley of firepower interrupted my thoughts. Windows blew out. Glass rained down. I had my radio out and changed the frequency to the one the local cops use. I screamed into it. "Machine-gun fire. One of us is down. Walter Laakso's place. Ambulance. Help."

The blood was draining from Kitty's face and heading for the hole in her chest. I heard sirens wailing in downtown Stonely, calling in volunteers for an ambulance and the posse. Herb's Bar would be cleared out by now.

I hoped they wouldn't be too late.

"Stay with us, Kitty," I said. "Help is on the way." Her eyes were fluttering. I wasn't sure she heard me.

All was quiet outside. The shooter hadn't anticipated our radios and our ability to contact outside help from the hunting trailer. He had to be gone by now. Only a fool would hang around until the entire town arrived.

"Go, Gertie," Cora Mae said. "Get out of here. I'll stay with Kitty. They'll arrest you if they catch you here."

I'd thought of that. If our local law enforcement found me here, they'd haul me in. I'd be behind bars with Blaze. Kitty would be in the hospital, and Cora Mae couldn't even drive. Who would be left to save us?

"Go," Cora Mae ordered. "I'll tell them you ran after the person who shot Kitty."

Another thought crossed my mind and that one got me fired up for flight. Cora Mae would have full access to George if I went to jail. Like I mentioned earlier, my mind does strange things under duress.

Sirens wailed and I estimated I had about two minutes, if that. I cautiously raised an empty glove in one of the windows and waited. Nothing. I stuck out my left arm thinking if I had to lose one it might as well be the one I didn't write with.

Nothing.

I grabbed my purse and glanced back at my friends down on the floor. Cora Mae was cradling Kitty's head.

When I opened the trailer door, a note was taped to the outside of it. *Just a warning,* it said.

I looked at the blood covering my two friends and thought it had been much more than a warning.

TWENTY-THREE

As I've said before, we love our weapons in the U.P. Most of us have at least three or four. Some of us have dozens. Automatic weapons might be illegal in this country, but Yoopers never consider themselves bound by the same laws as other United States citizens. We do what we want to.

Me? I had my purse full of weapons, but they only worked up close. That wasn't good enough. Than I remembered Grandma Johnson's pistol. I'd taken it away from her the last time she waved it around in the air, threatening me and my dog.

The run from the trailer to Walter's rusty junker was the longest of my life. There's not much scarier than the potential of a shot in the back by a hidden sniper. Every second I expected to feel the impact of a riddle of bullets ripping into my torso. While I started the truck, I anticipated someone out there beading into my forehead with a scope. My hands shook, fumbling with the ignition.

I blew out of Walter's driveway, still alive. Half a mile down the road, I spotted something resembling a big bear ahead of me. As I approached, I realized it was Fred running along the side. He was heading home, the smart boy.

After a mutually warm greeting, Fred hopped into the truck and we raced home to pick up Grandma's pea shooter. It wouldn't stand against the kind of weapon that was used at the trailer, but it was better than nothing.

I couldn't stop thinking about the bullet hole in Kitty and the color draining from her face.

The guinea hens did their little alarm dance around the truck until I stepped out and they recognized me. Fred dashed for the house, only two steps ahead of flapping wings and pointy beaks. The door wasn't locked. I opened it, we stepped in, and I instantly smelled old lady.

"What are you doing here?" I said to Grandma Johnson, who stood over the sink eating an orange in drippy bites. "You don't belong in my house."

"I've been waiting for you," the she-devil said, wiping her chin with her fingers. "Sit down. I'll get you a cup of coffee."

"I don't have time to chitchat," I said. "I'm picking up a few things. Then I'm gone."

"I need to say my piece," Grandma said. "I went to bingo last night with Pearl and she set me straight. As hard as it is, I'm apologizing to you for everything I did."

What a shock. My mother-in-law had never, ever admitted wrongdoing in all the years I'd known her.

"I'm sorry I got you in trouble," she said, easing down at the kitchen table and looking at her hands. "Our family is pulled apart because of me. Blaze in jail, you on the run, me without a home." At that, she gazed up at me with baleful eyes.

By now, I was hearing sirens in the distance, coming from every direction. Dickey and his deputies would comb the woods searching for the person who shot Kitty. They'd also be looking for me, but they'd assume I was on foot.

Eventually, they'd stop here to tell Grandma and Star that I was missing, lost in the woods, or worse. I had plenty of time before that happened.

"Kitty's been shot," I said. "I don't know if she's going to live."

Grandma gasped. "What happened?"

I gave her a rough outline. "There's a very bad person who is getting desperate," I said, after finishing. "I need to stop the killings and get my son out of jail. As much as you'd like to think that I'm a renegade criminal, I'm not. You and I are on the same side. We want the same things."

"Okay. I can see that now."

I didn't know whether to trust her or not. Grandma Johnson hadn't displayed any signs of humanity in all these years. Why would she start today?

"What can I do to help?" Grandma asked.

"You can tell Dickey Snell you haven't seen me."

"Never cared for that kid."

"And don't believe anything he tells you about me. If he says I'm lost in the woods, don't be alarmed. Okay?"

"Okay."

"And take care of Fred while I'm gone."

Grandma twitched. "That's expecting pretty much."

"And no hitting him with the fly swatter."

Grandma groaned and looked down at Fred with a distrustful glare before switching to her old helpless lady face to gaze at me. "Anything to help," she said. "I want to get back in your good graces and have my family together like before. I'd like to see us all together at the supper table. Does this mean I can stay?"

What could I say? She was ninety-two and trying to turn over a new leaf.

"You can stay," I agreed, knowing I'd regret it soon enough.

———

All of Tamarack County's law enforcement agents were busy over at Walter's house, so the jail wasn't guarded. Blaze was lying on a cot. When he saw me rummaging through desk drawers, he popped right up. "Look in the top right one," he said, good-guessing my intentions.

I found the key and opened the cell.

"This is crazy," I said. "You didn't kill Bob Goodyear or steal money from the credit union. I didn't either. So why are you in jail? And why am I on the run?"

"What's that thing on your head?" Blaze was staring at my blond hair.

"A disguise."

"What's all the commotion I'm hearing?" Blaze said, sounding pretty normal.

"Someone shot Kitty."

"Hell's bells," he roared. "I need to get my job back and help you hunt for whoever did this. Is she dead?"

"No. At least I don't think so."

"You need my help."

I had to remind myself that Blaze wasn't much of a criminal catcher even before the disease struck him down. But Dickie was far worse. The kid's college education hadn't taught him common sense or street smarts. Going by the book is a bad plan way up in the north woods.

"Here's a badge," I said to Blaze, handing him the one I had ordered for myself and watching him pin it on his shirt. "You're the sheriff as far as I'm concerned. Let's go."

"Where are we headed?"

I looked at my son. "I have absolutely no idea," I answered.

TWENTY-FOUR

TUESDAY STARTED OUT COLD and rainy. Blaze and I were holed up in an old-fashioned motel on the far side of Escanaba, less than half a mile from the hospital. The motel had twelve units and each one had its own entry. The heater below the window rattled continuously and condensation formed on the pane above it. Any colder and the rain would turn to snow.

We still didn't have much news on Kitty, except that she hadn't died through the night. At Cora Mae's last update, Kitty had survived through the surgery, but it was wait-and-see.

The TV6 morning news anchor had a bucket load of live updates, as well as last night's news regarding the backwoods shooting. Cameras rolled as an ambulance unloaded Kitty at the hospital's emergency entrance. More coverage of the local sheriff's attempt to apprehend a suspect.

"We've ascertained that the suspect fled through the woods," Dickey had said on TV, puffing up for the camera. "Wanted criminals were hiding in a trailer on Walter Laakso's property in Stonely.

Mr. Laakso has cooperated fully with the investigation. There's no reason to believe he knew anything about his unwelcome guests. We believe that the shooter was known by the victim, but that has not been confirmed, since the victim remains unconscious at this time."

The same photo of me appeared on the screen and Blaze chuckled. "What a bad picture," he said.

"I'll be sure to send them a better one when I find time."

"Gertrude Johnson," the anchor said, "is wanted for questioning in the death of Detroit native Robert Goodyear. Please contact the authorities if you see her. Do not approach her. I repeat, do not approach. She is assumed to be armed and dangerous."

Unbelievable what the media would say and do to sensationalize a story.

Blaze quit smiling when his own mug flashed on the screen.

"Bonnie and Clyde couldn't have captured the Upper Peninsula's imagination with any more color," the anchor said. "Witnesses saw a blond woman assisting Blaze Johnson in a breakout from the Stonely jail last night, fueling the flames of a rumor that the Johnson family masterminded the robbery of tens of thousands of dollars from Stonely's credit union. The blond Bonnie Parker hasn't been identified yet, but authorities are questioning witnesses and hope for a break in the case soon. This is TV6 live. Stay tuned for more updates."

After a commercial break, they interviewed Grandma Johnson. I watched through little slits between my fingers while holding my breath. "You pissants must have something better to do than scare an old lady to death, coming around here, leaping out of trucks. I should sic my dog on you. If my favorite daughter-in-law or my grandson are hiding, it's cuz you people like to tell lies to sell more papers. I oughta hit you with my fly swatter."

I wondered why she had the thing in her hand in the first place, since she wasn't supposed to hit Fred with it. I should have taken it with me when I had the chance. I also wondered how she got away with saying pissants on TV without getting bleeped.

Blaze and I sat in the motel room all morning staring at the television set, waiting for word on Kitty, and talking about what to do next.

"I can't sit here any longer," I said eventually, when we still didn't have a plan. "I need a new wig and you aren't exactly easy to miss. We have to figure out a disguise for you, too."

The only thing going our way right now was Blaze's condition. I hadn't seen any signs of abnormalities in his thinking process.

When we left the motel, I found a care package from Cora Mae on the passenger seat of Walter's truck. A black ball cap and a stick-on mustache for Blaze and the black flip wig for me—the one Kitty had been wearing when she got shot. I combed through it with my fingers. Images of last night kept flashing through my mind. Her lying on the floor, blood everywhere, Cora Mae holding her in her arms.

I wanted to kill someone.

Maybe the news guy was right. I was definitely armed and maybe I *was* dangerous.

My radio sprang to life while Blaze and I were on our way to Stonely. "Muffin Cakes," I heard and smiled. It was Sweet Cheeks. "Are you safe?" he asked.

"Sure," I answered. "Any new news?"

"Not much other than the entire town has been mobilized. I offered to scout around in Escanaba. That's my territory."

"Be careful. I hear your target is armed and dangerous."

"Always has been," he said before signing off.

How would I survive without my friends? I could kick myself in the hind end for doubting Cora Mae. Jealousy can twist a person until they are barely recognizable. Kitty, Cora Mae, and George were the best friends a girl could have. And my family? Well, that was another story. But Grandma Johnson hadn't blown my cover when she talked to the news reporters. Because of that, they might be still searching for me out in the woods.

I yawned from behind the wheel. We passed along the corridor leading from Escanaba to Gladstone with the bluff on one side and Lake Michigan on the other. A crisscross of train tracks lay ahead. We zipped past parked train cars and turned left on M35, windshield wipers pounding on high against the rain.

I yawned again. Sleep is my favorite hobby, especially on a day like today when it's overcast and rainy. I love to sleep more than anything, and I wasn't getting enough. I never learned to function on just a few hours. I get crabby. That's the only explanation I can give for why I'd go into Ruthie's Deer Horn Restaurant in broad daylight and draw on Tony Lento.

He sat at the counter, swiveled with his back to it, eating a sandwich and sharing a joke. Carl and Otis were telling tales at a table in the middle of the room, and Tony was chewing and listening. It was almost the end of the lunch run so at least the restaurant wasn't packed with witnesses to my madness. Carl and Otis knew me well enough and I hoped they liked me more than they liked Dickie Snell. They might not tell him what I did next.

I had left Cora Mae's black wig in the car and went in as myself. Blaze followed me, even though I'd expressly ordered him to stay in the truck. But he has my genes, so it's hard to tell him anything if his mind's already made up.

"Hey, Gertie. Hi, Blaze," Carl said as though it was just another day at Ruthie's and we weren't wanted by the law. "Pull up a chair. Otis is telling me about the tom turkey he tried to shoot."

"Dang thing came after me," Otis said. "That was one prehistoric reptile, he was big as a T-rex. Did you hear from the newspaper that turkeys descended from dinosaurs? You'd know it was true if you saw this one lift up and come at me. Claws the size of a pitchfork."

"What'd you do?"

"Ran in the house."

Tony watched me out of the corner of an eye. Ruthie came in from the kitchen carrying a coffeepot. "Gertie, gee, I never expected to see you in here today."

"I can't stay away from your good cooking," I replied, my eyes never leaving Tony. "We'll have something quick to take with us, something that doesn't need time to cook."

Ruthie poured coffee into two tall Styrofoam cups and packed up a whole cherry pie from behind the cash register. "Looks like snow soon," she announced. "I think I see a few flakes. Spring is going to have to wait. Hope it doesn't kill the daffodils before they get a chance to bloom."

"Daffodils are tough," I said. "They'll make it."

I paid up, and Blaze picked up our order from the counter. That's when I pulled Grandma's handgun from my purse and laid it against Tony's temple just like in the movies.

"Keep your hands where I can see them," I said. "I'm a little jittery from lack of sleep. I don't want to blow your brains out before I'm good and ready."

"Holy smokes, Gertie," Carl said.

"Be quiet, Carl."

Tony's eyes weren't shifty anymore. They were wide open. He tried to talk without moving his mouth. The "I'm so handsome" grin wasn't on his face. "What the hell are you doing?"

I could have asked myself the same thing. Other than his extra marital activities and accusations that he'd planted evidence from a woman I didn't trust, I didn't have anything on him. And last I heard cheating wasn't a killing offense, although it ought to be.

It felt good to see sweat beading on his forehead.

I pushed the barrel of the gun against his head just a little bit more. "If my friend dies," I said. "So do you."

"Do you know who you're threatening?" Carl stammered. "Tony's done a lot for our community. You're over the top now, Gertie. Maybe it's that change of life thing, you know, that women go through when they get older."

Blaze just stood by the door with our bag of goodies, watching the action. The sheriff's badge on his chest gleamed. I'd parked the truck where the restaurant's diners couldn't see it. "Go, Blaze," I said. "I'm right behind you."

I kept an eye on every man in the room. Ruthie, I could trust. She was one of my species, and would let this play out.

"Tony," I said. "Anything you want to tell me before I squeeze the trigger? Anything at all?"

He licked his lips and thought it over. "No," he said. "If I tell you what you want to hear, it'd only be a lie. Is that what you want? Or do you want the truth?"

"The truth works."

"The truth is that I don't know any more than you do."

I let him live in spite of an itch in my trigger finger. My bluff didn't work. Or else he was telling the truth. Or else he had nerves of steel.

Later in the truck, I began shaking so hard I almost drove into the ditch. Blaze had to take over. What was I thinking to put a gun to another human being's head? The worst thing was that it felt good. I enjoyed it! What was I capable of? What if I had lost control? What if I had pulled the trigger?

Then I thought of my friend. She might be dead right this minute.

It made me want to kill somebody all over again.

———

"I'm not taking them," Blaze said to Mary, after a long embrace and a lot of explanation.

"The doctors say you have to," she replied, trying to hand me six little brown bottles of medication.

"Why is he taking all of these?" I wanted to know.

"Two are so he doesn't have seizures. This one's supposed to knock out the infection in his head, this one's for pressure in his brain. I'm not sure about the other two."

"He seems perfectly fine to me," I said. "Better than when he was taking them."

"I never had any seizures," Blaze said.

"No, you didn't. But you might." Mary would never challenge a doctor on any medical decision. I don't have the same blind faith in them that she does. In my opinion, a current bad patient is a future live patient.

To make Mary happy, I took the bottles of pills. We'd decide later whether Blaze needed them. I'd seen very few signs of illness since we'd been hiding out together. Mainly little signs that indicated he didn't remember everything that he should.

The family had been warned that even when he was well he might have trouble differentiating between the realness of his nightmares and reality. The lines could blur, and they had. Imagine waking up from your worst nightmare and believing it really happened!

"How are you doing?" I asked Mary.

"I'm fine."

"How's Fred?"

"He's out back. With Grandma Johnson inside your house and the guineas outside, he decided to move in over here."

I ran outside in the rain and there he was. Fred came running like he was about to fling all hundred-plus pounds at me. He tried to stop at the last second, but I landed on the ground anyway. Fred towered above, lapping at my face.

I came up wet and happy.

Blaze bagged some clothes, kissed Mary, all the time ignoring her protests that he should turn himself in, that he wasn't well enough yet. We set out, leaving Mary crying in front of their house.

Blaze and I had chosen this path, and there was no turning back until the end of the road. We didn't have a choice. We'd committed.

Fred leapt past Blaze when he opened the truck's door and refused to budge. He rode between us.

TWENTY-FIVE

"WHO KNEW YOU WERE in Walter's trailer?" Blaze asked.

"George and Walter," I said. "That's it, besides the three of us inside."

"You've been talking on the radio."

"That's how we keep in touch. We have our own frequency."

"Frequencies are open to the public."

"That's why we have code names."

"Quit using the radios. Throw them away," Blaze said. "Someone's been listening in. You're lucky you aren't all dead. Hand it over."

My son threw the radio out the window and we drove along in silence, listening to the windshield wipers and watching rain turn to snow. Enormous flakes blotted out my view. "Better pull over," Blaze advised. When I did, he got out and came around to my side. "I'll take it from here."

"I'm driving just fine," I said.

"My memory's coming back," he said, pushing me over. "You don't have a driver's license."

I should have given him the medications, kept him soaring in outer space. "Have a pill," I said, holding up one of the bottles. He ignored me.

Blaze was wanted as a murder suspect. He had let me and Kitty escape while beading on the acting sheriff, had even put Dickey behind bars, and finally had broken out himself and was hanging with another wanted criminal.

And he was worried about a driver's license?

———

Lyla was out in front of the Gladstone salon, taking a break from doing customer's nails by smoking a cigarette. Blaze dropped me off around the corner, and I walked up to her.

She gave me a surprised stare, took one long, deep drag, and ground out the cigarette under her shoe. "Stay away," she said, smoke curling from her nose. "I can't be seen with you."

"I have a few questions, then I'll go."

Lyla glanced around, moving closer to the side of the building. "You're wanted by the cops."

"Believe me, I know. I heard about you and Tony. I'm sorry."

"Me, too. Everybody who knows Tony loves him, but they don't see what he's like at home. He's an entirely different person then, nothing like the easy guy others see. Him and me? We're through."

I didn't know what to say. I could have told her things to solidify her decision to leave, but she was hurting enough without more bad news.

"When you and Tony were serving beer at the dance the night Bob Goodyear was killed," I said, "did you see anything suspicious? Did you see anyone go outside? Hear anything unusual?"

Lyla shook her head. "I don't remember anything that would make a difference. Look, I know you want to get Blaze off, but maybe he did it. Did you ever think of that? Everybody knows what he went through with the meningitis, and we all saw how he wasn't right in the head afterwards."

I sighed as snow covered the top of my head. That's what they all would say. That Blaze hadn't been in his right mind and had killed the guy in the parking lot. He'd have to plead insanity and hope it stuck. Not to mention that I might go down with him.

"You heard about Kitty?" I asked. "She's near death because a killer opened fire on her. Blaze was in jail when it happened. How do you explain that?"

"I have a client in a few minutes. You better go."

Lyla hurried inside, glancing over her shoulder to make sure I wasn't following her in.

I was wasting my time. Every single person at the dance had the opportunity to slip outside unnoticed and kill Bob. I didn't even see Dave at all while I was there. Sue disappeared from the table when I went to get her a beer. Tony or Lyla could have taken breaks from pouring beers. When it came right down to it, the entire community was suspect. I needed to work a new angle—one that would pay off fast.

I walked down to the corner and looked both ways. The truck wasn't in sight. But Tony Lento was. He ran across the street right at me. I did another rapid scan for the truck. Where were Blaze and Fred?

Tony had his hands in his coat, making me wonder if he had a concealed weapon. But then I remembered where I was. This was the Michigan Upper Peninsula, Gladstone, to be exact, not Detroit or Chicago. I had mobsters on the mind. Nobody got mowed down on our streets.

He stopped in front of me and smiled. "I need a word with you, Gertie."

"I'm standing right in front of you, make it quick."

"What if I told you right here and now that I did it all? That I masterminded the robbery." Tony's smiling face was too close for comfort. "The robbery, the killings, the whole works? What would you say?"

"I'd believe it," I said, narrowing my eyes and thinking about the gun in my purse and the recording unit that wasn't turned on. I shuffled around, trying to get a hand in my purse to start the machine, but he clamped a strong, painful hold on my arm and didn't let go.

"What would you do with that information?" he hissed, no longer smiling. "I bet you'd call up Sheriff Snell and lay it all out for him."

"That would be a good start." And, I thought, I'd make a citizen's arrest, clamp handcuffs on you right this minute. My purse contents are wonderful. Talk about prepared. Now if Blaze would show up and hold Tony while I cuffed him, we'd be in business.

"Let's see," he snarled, showing me the side of him that he hid from the public, the side Lyla had mentioned a few minutes ago. "It would be my word against yours. Who would our good sheriff believe? You? I coach baseball every summer, make donations to all the local events, and go to church every Sunday. You're nothing but a crackpot with an addled son and a dysfunctional family."

I kept my face impassive and hard, but his words had shocked me. Just wait, I thought, Lyla's throwing you a curve ball. We'll see whose family is more dysfunctional. I envisioned slapping handcuffs on him and hauling him in, throwing him in a cell, tossing away the key.

Dickey wouldn't listen to me if I brought in Tony. He'd add new charges to my growing list of crimes. He'd book me for assaulting Tony.

Our truck turned toward me, two blocks down. I had to get away from this slime bucket before he saw our mode of transportation. Walter's truck was the only reason we were still on the road working the case.

"I'll get you eventually," I said.

Tony laughed. "You don't have a single piece of concrete evidence."

He continued laughing like he'd just heard a world-class joke. I trotted toward the truck, making small, stealthy motions, which Blaze picked up on. He turned away from Delta Avenue, parked, and waited for me to get in the truck a few minutes later.

"Tony's our man," I said to Blaze, trying to dodge a torrent of kisses from Fred. "He confessed."

I told Blaze about my conversations with Lyla and Tony. "He's right, you know," Blaze said. "What you think you know isn't worth much if you can't back it up."

Snow continued to fall while we drove to Escanaba to our motel hole-in-the-wall. I had learned a lot from living life on the wrong side of the law. The latest truth worried me the most.

Once I acquired outlaw status, my word became about as good as a roll of toilet paper.

TWENTY-SIX

I HAVEN'T SEEN THE story in the paper yet," I said first thing Tuesday morning to Laura DeLand over the motel phone.

"My boss killed it," she said, with genuine regret in her voice. "I tried hard. Sorry."

"Did he say why?"

"I have to substantiate the information you gave me before we can print it."

"In other words, they don't believe me."

"That's one way of putting it. I haven't given up. I'll keep working it."

"How's your houseguest?"

"She's okay."

"I'd like to come by and visit sometime soon."

"Anytime. That's the beauty of my job. I have the power to protect my sources."

Laura DeLand was smart and sweet, but she was young and still had fantasy-land visions of how the world was supposed to work.

She'd learn soon enough that no one was safe from suspicion or prosecution. Not even a news reporter. Not even a life-long sheriff like Blaze. Not even an innocent widow like me.

We still didn't have a new update on Kitty, but we had one on Cora Mae.

"I have a date with Kitty's doctor," she said from the center of my bed, fluffing the pillow and grinning. "A doctor. Can you believe it?"

"Sure," I said. "You're hot. Why wouldn't he want to go out with you?"

"We're going to have dinner in Marquette, then David's taking me to the Ojibwa casino to teach me roulette."

She bounced to a sitting position and rummaged through a tote bag. "I brought you more disguises." Cora Mae held up one of her black man-hunting stretch outfits. Spandex stuff looks great on her, but makes me feel like a stuffed sausage. "And heels." She hauled out little strappy things.

I shot her a look.

"You have to play the part," she advised. "What good is changing your hair color if you still look like Gertie Johnson from the neck down? I'll paint your toenails for you."

Fred chose that moment to leap on the bed and settle next to her. Blaze came out of the bathroom and plopped in a chair in front of the TV.

"Glamorous life we're leading," I said, watching Cora Mae layer red polish on my toes. "Actually, it's the pits. We have to sneak around. And we worry all the time about someone identifying us. We aren't accomplishing a thing besides racking up more charges against us. It's only a matter of time."

"Quit whining," Cora Mae said. "It could be worse. We could be lying in the hospital with Kitty, riddled with bullets."

"Or in the morgue," Blaze added.

In the bathroom, I changed into the clothes that were supposed to make me into someone new. Then Cora Mae and I drove to the grocery store. She went inside and purchased food from a list I had given her. After that, we went to the hospital to visit Kitty.

No question about it, I was taking a risk by going in, but I couldn't stay away. The last image I had of my friend wasn't a pleasant one. I needed to replace it with one of her on the way to a full recovery.

Cora Mae had been by her side through the entire tragedy, so the intensive care nurses didn't pay any attention when we walked past the nurse's station.

"She's on a respirator," I gasped when I saw Kitty. Tears were welling in my eyes. "No one told me that. Can't she breathe on her own? You should have told me."

"I thought I had." Screens were flashing numbers and squiggly lines, monitoring her life. We sat for a while without any movement from Kitty, no sign that she was alive, the respirator wheezing away. Murderous thoughts replaced the sadness.

I had to stay free until the person who did this was brought to justice. I wanted to shoot his eyes out. "What kind of slime would do something like this?" I said. But it was just a rhetorical question. Cora Mae didn't have an answer.

George came in a little later, grinning widely when he saw the new me. He opened his mouth, closed it, shook his head.

"Well, say it," I said.

"I don't know quite what to say."

"Tell her she's beautiful," Cora Mae said. "A woman likes to hear that when she's changed her style."

"Almost didn't recognize her. That's for sure."

"This isn't permanent," I said.

George gave me a hug. We stayed a little longer without detecting any changes in Kitty's condition. Then we went our separate ways.

———

Blaze was pacing the floor like a madman when I got back from the hospital. His hair was standing on end and he really looked like he'd lost it. He reminded me of the threat some of the local parent's used with their children when they were naughty. "Knock it off," they'd warn them, "or I'll send you to Newberry." Everyone knew what that meant. Until 1990, Newberry, the moose capital of Michigan, also was home to the U.P.'s famous Newberry psychiatric hospital. Now it was a prison. Blaze and I might end up in Newberry after all.

"They found the vehicle," Blaze said. "It was on the news."

I bit my lip. How did Dickey manage to find his truck so fast? We should have had months, maybe even years before anyone discovered it at the bottom of the lake. "It was bound to happen sooner or later," I said.

He stared at me. "What are you talking about?"

That brought me up. I never told Blaze about the sheriff's truck's final resting place. "What are *you* taking about?" I shot back at him.

"Tony Lento's car. They pulled it out of the Escanaba River right over where Pa died."

"How do you know that?"

"The news." Blaze jerked his head toward the television set and resumed pacing. "He went off the road. The car fell at least thirty-five feet."

I cut the sound on the TV with the remote. "Did they find his body?"

"Not yet, but you know how the river is. They're bringing in divers."

The upper Escanaba River was wide and rocky. The current, especially now in the spring, was swift and strong. Tony's body could have been carried downstream in the rapids.

I fell onto the sagging motel bed next to Fred, face first. I laid there motionless. My Barney used to fish for trout along that section of the river, hauling out browns, brooks, and rainbows. Everyone other than Blaze and me thought he'd died in his waders of a heart attack, because that's what we told them. The truth was he'd stepped into a hole, his waders filled up, and he drowned. Barney was a proud man and would have been horrified if all of Tamarack County knew the truth.

I could hardly bear to think of Barney's last moments under the high water or the terror he must have experienced when he realized he wouldn't escape the death trap. I didn't have quite the same compassionate thoughts for Two-Time Tony, but I still was shocked by the news.

Envisioning the bridge above the river was easy. I'd been back to the site several times, reliving the horror, talking to Barney.

Then I had a horrible thought. What if Tony had faked his own death? Maybe he had the money and he wanted to make a clean start someplace warm with his little chickadee? He could have pushed the car over the top of the bridge and made his escape in a get-away car.

I rubbed Fred's ears while I thought. Where did that leave Blaze and me? Up the creek without a paddle, so to speak. Tony was the sneakiest, snakiest man I'd ever had to deal with. What a way to throw the whole town into stunned mourning when all along they should have been building a hanging scaffold and tying a noose.

And what about Lyla? She was fed up, but she must still have feelings for him. How could he leave her like that, thinking he was dead? I had a repertoire of nasty names to call him. If only he was right in front of me.

I considered appealing to Dickey's common sense, groveling at his feet, and hoping he'd listen. By the time I went to sleep, I decided it was the right thing to do. It was a good thing I waited until the next day to turn myself in. By then I'd changed my mind.

TWENTY-SEVEN

BLAZE HAD A BAD night. His old suspicions came back and it took all my persuasive reasoning to keep him in the motel room. Our family spent months helplessly watching him fight the infection in his brain. We still didn't know how it developed. Was it something that came out of the ground? Was it airborne? A wood tick? We'd never know the answer.

We were lucky to have him back. Most people die from meningitis.

I gave him a few dollars to count and stack and that kept him happy for a while. But the night was long and hard. Enemies came at him from all sides. They were at the windows, at the door, behind the shower curtain. I didn't tell him how close to the truth he really was.

I started to suspect that he had more paranoid symptoms when he grew tired. All the drama was wearing on him. So Wednesday morning, Cora Mae knocked quietly on our motel door and tiptoed in to watch over him. She looked tired from her hot doctor date, but happy as she snuggled under my bed covers. I left Blaze snoring away, dead to the world.

Fred opened an eye, but seemed content where he was curled on the floor.

Then I went over the edge after Tony.

———

According to TV6 news, the search for Tony's body had followed the Escanaba River toward the river's mouth in Escanaba where it ended at Lake Michigan. Nightfall had hampered their efforts, so they were at it again today, working their way down.

The investigation on the upper end was complete. No body yet.

I parked the car a ways beyond the broken rail where the car had left the road. I changed from heels to sneakers, combed through the black bob with my fingers, and started down to the river. The view from the top used to be breathtakingly beautiful. After Barney's death, I couldn't see its beauty anymore.

The trip down is steep and rocky, without any visible path. I had to clutch at brush to keep from falling, but finally I stood at the bottom, scanning out over the river for signs of Tony's car. Dickey must have had it removed yesterday, but I could still focus on the angle of projection and make a guess as to where it landed, smack in the middle.

The current rode high and mighty, swirling and slapping against the rocky shore at my feet. If Tony had been inside the car, he was dead. If he hadn't been inside, I wondered how he would have pulled it off. The car had to be traveling at more than an idle to break through the barrier up above. How do you get a car up to speed on the road, jerk it to the proper angle for impact, and get out of the way before it goes over?

Quite a trick. He had to be a desperate man to even attempt it.

I poked around, keeping one eye on the road above in case company joined me. Nothing worthwhile surfaced. I walked along the riverbank, studying the ground for clues, anything out of the ordinary. Nothing.

That's when I drove over to the jail to turn myself in and take my chances with the legal system, the one I've been in conflict with all my life. Anything to do with the government sits poorly with most of our community and that includes me. Having Blaze as sheriff was tolerable because he bent the rules once in awhile, looked the other way if he felt it was right. Blaze really cared about the community. But Dickey Snell? He reminded me of why we dislike government.

No one was there. So I took off the wig and went to Ruthie's for a piece of pie.

Otis was the only other customer in the Deer Horn. He flung his hands over his head in a gesture of surrender. "Don't draw on me, Gertie," he said. "I'll admit to anything you want me to, just don't shoot." Otis had a grin on his face.

"There must be something illegal about parking a train someplace other than in a train station," I quipped back. "I'll have to shoot you twice for that infraction. Ruthie, I need a pot of coffee and a piece of cherry pie. That last one was delicious."

"To go?"

"No, I'll eat it here." I sat down next to Otis. "Where is everybody?"

"Hunting for Tony," Ruthie said. "Have you heard about his accident?"

"Yup."

"It's a terrible thing," Otis said. "That's the second car that's gone off in that spot in the last five years. It's slippery along there when it's raining."

"Did you guys call the cops after I came in and threatened Tony?" I said, cutting into the pie.

"Naw," Otis said. "It woulda been bad for Ruthie's business."

I hadn't thought of that. No one wants to eat in an establishment where there's a shooting risk attached to it.

"Strange though," Otis scratched at the side of his face like it helped his thought process. "Tony didn't call them either. He smoothed himself out and finished his sandwich without even mentioning that it happened."

"It's leaking out," Ruthie said. "Onni Maki came in earlier and asked me if it was true. I told him he shouldn't believe everything he hears."

"I'm sorry for the trouble," I told her. "I don't know what got into me."

"That's okay. It added some excitement to the day. I wonder why they haven't found Tony's body yet." Ruthie flipped on a little TV behind the counter. She checked for news, found none, and left it on with the volume low. "Want anything else, Gertie?"

"Just keep the coffee fresh," I replied, thinking I'd sit there until Dickey discovered me, see how long it took him. "I'm turning myself in."

"How come?" Otis said. "It's been real exciting around here with you on the loose."

"Not quite as exciting for me. I can't do any more on my own. I'm out of ideas."

"We're rooting for you," Ruthie said. "We know you and Blaze didn't do anything wrong."

"I'm hoping that if I tell Dickey what I know, he'll be able to use it to crack the case."

Otis humphed like he didn't believe it.

"It was Tony scheming all along," I said, going on to tell them what I thought had happened. "By now he's getting off a plane in Brazil. He's left me holding the bag, and I don't have the resources to stop him. The law has a longer arm."

"Poor Lyla," Ruthie said. "Either way, dead or living in Brazil, Tony's gone and it's going to be painful for her. How's she going to keep that big house on a manicurist's salary?"

George came in at that moment, did a double-take, and sat down at the table with Otis and me. After getting George coffee and pie, Ruthie sat down, too. I told George what I was up to.

"I guess it's for the best," George said. "I'll get you a good lawyer, try to get you out on bail. I'll even put my house up for you if that's what it takes."

"You're a good man, George." I held his hand then, right in front of Otis and Ruthie. If I was going to jail, it might be a long time before I had that warm, comforting hand in mine again. "Take care of my dog for me while I'm gone."

"Maybe after all this is cleared up," George said, "we can talk about us and where we want to go from here."

Ruthie's eyes got wide. I blushed.

"Look at that!" Otis shouted, knocking his chair over and rushing behind the counter to turn up the volume on the TV.

As it happened, Tony wasn't stepping off an airplane in an exotic country with a suitcase filled with cash. Diver's working close to the Escanaba dam brought him up to the surface right about noon.

Tony Lento had turned up dead in the water.

The news got even worse from there. According to the breaking-news anchor, undisclosed evidence collected at the scene of the accident suggested foul play. Everyone at the table turned away from the television and stared at me. Even George.

They thought I was responsible!

I kicked back from the table and ran out the door, almost blinded by the tears flooding my eyes. I heard George calling my name, but I didn't turn back. He chased me to the truck, but I was quick, slamming and locking the door against him.

I kicked up gravel leaving the restaurant parking lot, nearly running George down. By the time I chanced a look back, he was a small dot in my rearview mirror.

TWENTY-EIGHT

I'D SEEN THEIR FACES after hearing the news. The unspoken questions. I'd threatened Tony's life in front of a restaurant filled with witnesses. I'd pulled out a handgun and planted it on the side of Tony's head. One irrational moment of tampering with evidence by taking the Glock off the ground had led to this.

Friends and acquaintances I'd known for almost a lifetime were turning against me. I saw it happen before my eyes. If my friends no longer believed me, who would? It was too late to turn myself in and hope for the best. I felt like Thelma and Louise all rolled into one, with exactly the same option staring me in the face.

Nowhere to run. Nowhere to hide.

Tampering with evidence, aiding and abetting in the murder of Bob Goodyear, breaking out of jail, destroying government property (Dickey's truck), threatening Tony with a weapon, and murder one for the killing of same. Had I left anything out? Anything at all? I might as well take the rap for the robbery, too.

Michigan didn't have the death penalty, but if they did, I'd be tried in a court of law, found guilty, and put to death like an old dog. Why had I messed everything up so badly? I should never have done any of the things I'd done. Kitty wouldn't be almost dead if it wasn't for me. My family would be sitting down in a few hours to a nice hot meal. I wouldn't even mind listening to Grandma Johnson crab, if I could only have things back the way they were.

Twenty miles outside of Stonely I pulled over and cried my eyes out in the back lot of a truck stop. I cried for all of us—especially Kitty and Blaze. After I stopped hiccupping, I felt better, splashed water on my face in the restroom, gassed up the truck wearing my disguise, and even found a phone, where I called the hospital to check on Kitty.

All they would tell me was that she was still in ICU.

I drove to Escanaba, scolding myself aloud for feeling sorry for myself. "You're tough as tacks," I said to me. "You're smart and brassy and you're supposed to be solving crimes, not committing them. Get a grip on yourself."

Flashing police car lights ahead had traffic backed up. The line edged along, moving slowly across Ludington Avenue, a few blocks from the motel. An accident of some sort? I craned my neck to see. A police officer waved traffic around what looked like a police convention up ahead. Walter's truck edged along with the rest until I was abreast of the motel.

My hole-in-the-wall was crawling with state troopers.

———

"Turn on the TV, quick," I ordered Grandma Johnson when she finally picked up the phone. I was two blocks from the motel, in the back of a place called Chuck's Bar.

"I have it on," she said. "This is better than soap operas. I've been glued to it so bad I almost wet my pants rather than miss something. I always told you she was trouble, but you wouldn't listen."

"What's happening?"

"Blaze was a good boy until he hooked up with her."

"Mary? What did Mary do?"

"Not Mary. That Cora Mae. She sweet-talked my grandson into a life of crime."

"Just tell me what's going on."

"It's on the TV right this minute. That boy with the cute hair is telling us about it. A motel manager got suspicious about certain activity in one of the rooms, so he called the authorities. They found Blaze and Cora Mae inside one of them. Can you imagine that? Mary's gonna just die."

"Cora Mae's strictly a friend."

"I'm sure she is," Grandma said, dripping sarcasm. "That's why she wore a blond wig and busted him out of the jail. She was Bonnie. And she's made him Clyde."

The wig! I'd left it in the motel room. The cops must think she was the one who was wearing it. Could this get any worse?

"What about Fred?"

"He ran off. I was watching him good just like I promised, but he kept running over by Mary. She musta fed him better. Then he disappeared. You have to believe me. I didn't hurt him."

"I know that. Wasn't he in the room with Cora Mae and Blaze?"

"Why would you worry about that rabid animal when your own son is in a heap of trouble?"

Someone up front by the bar flicked on an overhead screen. "You can go out in the street and watch it," someone called out. Someone else raised a beer. "But I'd have to leave my Bud behind."

"I've gotta go," I said to my mother-in-law.

I hung up while Grandma was still talking and settled in for a lesson in friendship. The anchor flipped back and forth, replaying the capture of Blaze and Cora Mae, then panning to another TV6 crew that was running around Stonely interviewing residents.

I found out who my friends were.

Sometimes what you discover surprises you. For example, Walter's my friend. He might be a tad eccentric with his shotgun greetings and morning happy hours, but he didn't tell the cops about the truck I was driving. They'd have me by now if he had.

Cora Mae and Kitty are at the top of my friend list. George, I can't even think about. I saw the uncertainty in his eyes, the doubt cast at me right along with Ruthie and Otis. Even Grandma came through when she had to.

I also found out who never really liked me, because those were the first ones to line up for the TV cameras. I could see Dave and Sue Nenonen in the background, waiting for the news reporter to introduce them. Sue was fussing with her hair to get it just right for her interview. Onni Maki, scrawny, self-proclaimed stud muffin, was at the microphone paying me back for the time I zapped him with my stun gun.

"Gertie Johnson was always a little off in the head," Onni said, trying for a seductive grin for any available women who might be watching. It made him look more like a convicted sexual predator than Romeo. "You can't do nothin' about bad genes," he said into the microphone. "Poor Blaze didn't have a fighting chance from the day he was born. They oughta take it easy on him cuz of his upbringing."

It was Dave's turn. "Every time she came into the credit union, I'd watch her close," he said. "She had a sneaky look about her, like she was looking for trouble. Well, she found it this time."

Sue stood next to her husband, stiff as a statue, her face frozen in terror. She was fighting a losing battle against a bad case of stage fright.

"Tell 'em, Honey," Dave said. "Tell them what she did."

Sue shook her head. Dave just stared at her until she said, "I ... I can't. You do i ... it."

"Okay," he said, turning back to the reporter. "When Sue heard on television about that blond wig, she put two and two together and came up with five. Someone came to our house impersonating a law enforcement official. Isn't that right, Honey?"

Sue was stricken. She couldn't even nod. Even her eyelids were frozen as she stared at the camera.

"Anyway," Dave said. "She's pretty sure it was Gertie Johnson under that wig, not Cora Mae. But they both could have used it for their own concerns. Can you believe it? Gertie's got a lot of brass to come right up to my house and question my wife."

"What kind of questions?" The newsman wanted to know.

Dave didn't bother letting Sue have the floor since she wasn't doing anything with it. "Gertie Johnson came over and impersonated a police officer. She said she was an officer from Sault Ste. Marie following up on the murder of that one guy."

There was another charge to add to my growing list of criminal offenses. Impersonating a police officer. I wondered how much time I'd get for that one.

"Anything else?" the reporter prompted.

"She made insinuating comments about my wife's million-dollar inheritance."

That sparked a reaction from Sue. Her head swiveled around to her husband and she frowned. "We weren't going to tell anybody that," she said. "And now you said it right on television, in front of the world. What's wrong with you?" She moved closer to him. If I was Dave, I'd start running. Sue had forgotten she was in front of a camera.

"But, Honey."

"Don't honey me." The camera operator must not have wanted the program to turn into some bawdy reality show, because he panned away from the dueling duo, following the news guy as he moved away from them.

"Thank you for coming forward," the news reporter said to Onni, who trailed behind him. "One last question. Do you have any idea where Gertie Johnson might have gone? It seems that she's disappeared from the face of the earth."

"I don't know where she's gone, but I know where she's going." Onni glared into the camera for effect. "Gertie Johnson is going to hell."

The reporter gave a weak laugh for the camera and said, "I assume you're talking about Hell, Michigan, otherwise we might have to censor you."

"You know exactly what I meant. She's goin—"

The story ended there. At least for me. I'd seen enough.

When I left the dark, smoky bar, the sun was still shining. I thought for sure it must be the middle of the night. So much had happened.

From the driver's seat of Walter's rusted-out truck, I considered the circumstances and my options. There weren't any choices available to me that I could readily see. I was almost out of cash, I didn't have anything to wear other than the man-hunting outfit Cora Mae duded me up in, and my spirit was gone.

How was I going to prove that Tony had killed Bob Goodyear if Tony was murdered? He couldn't confess, which seemed to be the only way I could possibly get out of this mess.

Wait a minute!

What was I thinking!

I had been so busy feeling sorry for myself and my friends that I overlooked a glaringly, obvious question.

Why had Tony been murdered? It was looking more and more like he had been part of a scheme, a ring of criminals. I had assumed Tony was the kingpin, but maybe not. Whoever murdered Tony knew the truth, and that truth could set me free, right along with all my friends and family that I had managed to get into such major trouble. Now all I had to do was locate that person and force a confession.

Simple, right?

Well, no, but it gave me direction and something even more important that I thought I'd lost. It gave me hope.

TWENTY-NINE

I HAD A WILD idea that I might find clues at Tony's turkey hunting blind. No real reason. It just popped into my head. "Go to Tony's hunting blind," my head ordered. I was back in private investigator mode, back to believing in intuition and luck.

When I came into the clearing, a flock of turkeys trotted for cover, all screeching the call they make when they're frightened. Turk-turk-turk. Tony's blind had a few creature comforts behind its exterior of straw bales. I sat down on a hunting stool and opened a small cooler. I found homemade jerky and one beer inside, and made hasty work of them both, since I was famished.

The forest was alive with bird chatter this late afternoon. A blue jay landed close by, looking for seeds. I saw one of the turkey scouts poke her head out from behind a stand of fir trees, one enormous, superwoman telephoto lens. She stared at the blind while I watched from a tiny hole in the straw. After a minute, she ducked back in the woods and disappeared.

The Upper Michigan backwoods is my favorite place to be. It's so alive. Aside from deer and turkeys, we have black bears, gray wolves, an occasional moose, red foxes, coyotes, cougars. And that's only a list of the large mammals. I could go on all day.

The air was still warm, the birds sang, and I lay down on some loose straw to rest. That's when my husband Barney decided to visit me again. I was so glad to see him, although I wished he'd show up the times I called out to him for guidance. He always did whatever he wanted, and that hadn't changed even with death.

Barney looked exactly the same as last time, he hadn't aged a bit in two years. More than I could say for myself. I'm surprised he recognized me in the clothes and wig I wore. But he sat down beside me, got comfy, and placed his hand on the side of my cheek like he used to do.

We didn't say anything for a while. I was afraid he would vanish if I uttered a single word. Finally, he spoke. "Everything is going to be all right," he said. "It'll work itself out like it always does."

"Can't you help me?" I said, as quietly as I could, so I wouldn't jar away the dream. "Give me some direction. A place to start. A glimpse into the future."

"You have to let go."

"Of you? Never."

"Of fear."

"I have quite a lot to be fearful about. Have you been paying attention to what's been happening lately?"

He smiled and I saw the old twinkle in his eye that he used to get when I amused him in some way. "You have so much love in you," he said. "Let it out. Trust your friends and family. They're all you have, but they're precious, the most important part of your life."

"These days it's hard to tell who's who."

"I think inside you know."

We stayed together like that. I could feel real warmth radiating from him even though I knew he was only a dream.

When I sat up he was gone. I remembered what he said to me, but I didn't understand a single word of it.

Night moves in fast in the forest. One minute the world was a soft gray. The next minute everything went dark. I heard the flapping of large wings, a rush of air, and an entire gang of gobblers and hens settled in the maple tree above me for the night.

What was Tony thinking to put his blind right under a roost? No skilled turkey hunter would do that. Turkeys like to roost together in the same spot every night. At first dark, when their eyesight starts to go, the whole bunch takes to their favorite tall tree.

A hunter needs to find out where they spend the night, then set up about a hundred yards off, hoping that when morning comes, they'll fly in that direction. He doesn't set up right under the roost.

That got me thinking about the whole point of Tony's turkey hunting blind. If he wanted a secure love nest, wouldn't he have picked something a little more comfortable, like a motel? I answered my own question. Maybe not. There's something exciting and romantic about the call of the wild. Maybe the woods brought out the animal in Tony. Besides, if someone had spotted his car in a motel parking lot, it would have been all over town within minutes. The only prying eyes out here didn't speak our language, so they couldn't tell on him.

197

Who was Tony seeing behind Lyla's back? That answer was important. I *had* to find out.

It was too dark to find my way out of the woods, which didn't matter much, since I had no place to go. If I wanted a safe house for the night, this was as good as any. And the price was right. I heard wings flap in alarm overhead when I rearranged some of the straw to keep warm, but they settled in again, confident that they were safe from predators for the night.

I slept well, knowing I was safe for at least a little longer, too.

————

At the first sign of dawn, the woods woke up. My turkey friends spotted me and left the tree in a hurry. I kicked around under a dead grove of elms and found a few morel mushrooms. They aren't quite as tasty raw and gritty with dirt, but I was hungry. Usually I like them sautéed in butter, but an investigator, aka the hunted, has to make do.

What I really needed was a shower and a change of clothes. I debated stopping at home for a few creature comforts, but rejected the idea. My home would be watched. My friends would be followed. That is, they might have been under surveillance, if they weren't all in the hospital or in jail.

What I couldn't do without was my morning coffee. I had the start of a caffeine headache, and it threatened to take me down harder than any flu virus could. I stumbled out of the woods, climbed into my truck, and drove to the only place I could think of going to.

The shades were still drawn and the door jamb was still pried loose where Tony had allegedly come in with the orange shoes. Nothing had changed at Shirley's house since the last time I'd been there. Dirty dishes still cluttered the sink. Not a single thing more had been packed up—almost as though Shirley had abandoned her life here all together.

I turned on Shirley's television, but it only had rabbit ears on the top of it and my channel surfing didn't produce anything newsworthy.

After that, I rummaged through cupboards and boxes and found what I needed. A shower later and the beginning of a second pot of coffee, and I felt human again. I even found workout clothes that fit me in one of the boxes. A dream come true for someone in my situation.

What even made it better? A working phone. Shirley hadn't turned off her utility services. Yippee. The tide was finally turning my way.

The hospital had Kitty listed as a patient, so she was still alive. No one would tell me anything more than that. I cursed the federal government for all its so-called privacy measures, when all of us knew we didn't have a bit of privacy from them.

I called Lyla next. "I'm going after the person who killed Tony," I said, quickly before she realized who she was talking to and hung up. "It won't cost you a dime. I need to clear my name."

"Everybody says you killed him, Gertie."

"You know I didn't. If I had, I would have shot him, not fixed it so he left the road above the river. You know that stretch of road isn't my favorite. Down below is where I lost Barney. Besides, I didn't even know where Tony was at the time he died."

Heck, I hadn't known where he was most of the time when I was supposed to be trailing him. Catching him in Ruthie's Restaurant had been a fluke. I had stumbled over him in one big accidental moment.

"I hope they don't start suspecting me next," she said. "Tony and I had a terrible fight at the salon. They'll blame me for his death, say I wanted to get rid of him."

She didn't sound too broken up over Tony's demise, but to be fair, she'd been through a lot of heartache with him.

"I'll clear both of us." The lie slid easily over my lips. If Lyla had anything to do with Tony's death, I'd turn her right in to free Blaze and Cora Mae. "Why did you suspect Tony of cheating in the first place? What made you hire the Trouble Busters?"

"It was only suspicions and feelings. I didn't know anything for fact."

"Did you have someone in mind? Someone you thought he was seeing?"

"I'd rather not say."

"How can I help you if you won't tell me what I need to know?"

"But I'm not sure, and I'd hate to start rumors."

"Who am I going to tell? I don't have a single friend left to gossip with."

"Okay, but keep it quiet. I don't know if it's true or not."

"I'll keep it to myself."

"Before I hired you, Tony was hanging around at the credit union more than usual. And one day, when I was shopping in Escanaba, I saw him in a restaurant and he was with a woman."

"Who was he with?"

"Sue Nenonen."

"But she helps with the books at the credit union and he's an accountant. It could have been strictly professional."

"Yes, that's true. And when you followed him, you didn't see him around the credit union or with Sue." I could hear in her voice how bad she wanted to believe in Tony's loyalty to her. "You didn't, did you?"

"No, I didn't."

Even now I couldn't tell Lyla about the tryst I'd semi-witnessed at the hunting blind. She needed to hold on to a few good memories of the cheating bum. If only I had kept my eyes on the blind instead of letting nature call, I'd know who the woman was. Had it been Dave's wife, Sue?

After reassuring Lyla that I'd do everything possible to catch Tony's killer, I replayed the tape I'd run in the woods while scooting on my belly.

"I don't believe you," the woman had said. The sound wasn't crisp and clear. She'd lowered her voice, and she was angry.

"I'll take care of it," Tony had said. "We'll be together soon."

"I've heard that before." Then giggling and they had made up the good old-fashioned way.

I played the tape back several times. Was Sue the woman in the woods?

I called Sue and Dave's home number, hoping Sue wasn't already at the credit union crunching numbers. She picked up the phone on the second ring.

"This is a representative for the Elizabeth Taylor perfume company," I said to her, holding the recording unit as close as possible to the receiver. I wished I had a telephone hookup for my recorder.

It would have simplified the process. "You've won a year's supply of *White Diamond* perfume."

"Is this a joke?" she asked. "I didn't enter a contest."

"Your significant other must have signed you up for the drawing."

"Dave?"

"Your significant *other*." I put enough emphasis on "other" to send the proper message. "You know what I mean."

Sue hung up.

I replayed the tryst talk from the woods, then my perfume contest chat with Sue, but the sound was garbled. I couldn't hear Sue at all. Remembering her voice from the few sentences she had uttered before hanging up, I didn't think she was the woman in the woods. But a person's voice is changed slightly both through a phone connection *and* when replayed on a recording unit.

I couldn't say absolutely positively that it wasn't Sue.

Now what?

I played the tape over and over until I was fairly certain I could identify the voice if I ever heard it again. Then I called Laura DeLand's house. "This is Laura," she said into her end of the phone when I asked for Laura.

"This is Gertie. I thought I'd stop by and talk to Shirley."

"She's gone. You just missed her."

"Gone as in moved? Or gone like to the store?"

"She left for Lower Michigan."

"But she didn't take any of her things from her house."

"How do you know that?"

"Well, I ... uh ... I'm there right now."

"WHAT?"

"I needed a place to stay." Something was wrong. I shouldn't have said that. Laura's tone changed from friendly and helpful to wary and cunning. Something else was wrong, too, but I couldn't place it.

"I'm sure she wouldn't want people in her house," Laura said. I could tell she didn't like it one bit. Was breaking and entering on my list of pending criminal charges yet? I couldn't remember.

"I was just leaving," I said. "Sorry to have missed her."

I sat and stared at the phone. Then I replayed the tape, listening hard to the woman's voice. Laura DeLand's voice was a dead-on match with the one from the woods.

THIRTY

I DIDN'T KNOW WHAT to do with my new insight. That sweet young reporter just couldn't have been dallying around with Tony Lento. She was beautiful. She could get any man she wanted. Why Tony? It had to be a mistake.

And why did I tell her where I was? Now I'd have to vacate my last remaining hideout. Or did I? She was a reporter. Was she required to protect me, or was it optional? I didn't know anything about news reporter ethics.

I calmed down and thought it through, but all I came up with were more questions. Were Tony and Laura planning to run away with the credit union's money? Did Bob kill Kent to keep him quiet? Did Tony kill Bob to silence him, too? Were the two lovebirds trying to set up Shirley by planting orange shoes in her house? Or was Shirley part of the scheme?

The most perplexing question of all might never be answered. Why did the robbers steal Monopoly money instead of real hundred dollar bills?

I turned off the coffeepot, but didn't try to cover my tracks by cleaning up. I had to confront Laura in person, force her to listen to the tape. She had some explaining to do. I'd get the truth out of her if I had to torture it out of her. I still had my weapons arsenal and I hadn't used my stun gun recently. My trigger finger was itchy.

———

I was backing out of the driveway when George pulled in behind me, blocking my escape. I stayed where I was, palming my pepper spray, while he strode up to the truck window. If he yanked the door open or made any other aggressive gesture, he was getting it full on, no holds barred.

"Dickey got a call-in tip a few minutes ago," he said through the crack I'd made in the window. "He's rounding up his volunteers and then he'll head over here."

"You came to warn me?" I could have cried. What a wonderful man. And I was about to assault him with my pepper spray!

George nodded. "I'll have to circle around and come back over with them, or else they might suspect something's up."

Laura hadn't wasted any time calling in the troops after she found out where I was. "I don't have any place to go," I said.

"Is it time to turn yourself in, Gertie? I'm sure we can find the truth."

"Never! Dickey's a dope. And I have a few loose ends that might tie up the entire case, if only I can work them."

"We don't have much time then. You need to go. Do what you have to do and meet me at my place later."

"I have a habit of ruining my friend's lives. I'm a curse. You don't want to get involved with me."

George grinned. "I can't wait to get involved with you. Now go."

"What happened to Fred?" I called out the window as he ran back to his truck.

"Fred's back home with Grandma."

"Look out for him. He's in hostile territory."

George backed up, clearing the way for my escape. One more time, I'd lucked out, turning away from the sound of sirens and blowing a cloud of dust up behind me. It would settle before they arrived. And Dickey would spend the rest of the day combing the neighborhood and lifting useless clues from Shirley's house.

As it turned out, I spent the rest of the day doing the same thing I suspected Dickey was doing. But instead of combing the woods, I was searching Escanaba for Laura DeLand. She wasn't at her house or at work. Either she was out on assignment, or she had skipped town.

After hours of wasted effort, I put myself in her shoes. Mentally, of course. What would I do if I were her? Where would I go? Then it hit me. She'd be in Stonely driving right behind the sheriff, getting first dibs on a breaking story and killing two birds with one stone. She'd tipped off the cops to my whereabouts, now she got to reap the rewards by writing the wrap-up story. Both a personal and a professional coup.

And I thought she was sweet.

If I ever got out of this mess, I'd have to improve my people analytical skills. My character judgment needed an overhaul. That's what being on the run does to a person. Before my criminal career,

I took trust for granted. Now, I couldn't find any reason to believe in anyone.

How could I have misjudged George so badly? He'd been a friend for years and years, and in one minute at Ruthie's restaurant, with one misinterpreted look from him, I had been ready to count him out as a true friend. Had I seen only what I wanted to see? Was I afraid of him, of my feelings for him, of closeness?

Driving back to Stonely to spend the night with George, I thought I understood Barney's words better. I didn't want to let go, like he'd advised me to do when we chatted at Tony's blind. Barney had been my life, and I was still hanging on with all my might. But he was right. I didn't have to forget him. And as he said, I *did* have a lot of love inside me. I just had to release a part of my life that would never come back, that was gone for good. I had to move on. Start living and loving again.

Tonight I was going to do it with the only other man I ever cared about.

George had a big pot of chili simmering on the stove. Its wonderful aroma would have bowled me over, but Fred beat it to the punch. What a surprise! George grabbed me as I fell backward while a two-ton black shepherd tackled me with slurpy, sloppy dog-breath kisses.

"Thank you, George," I cried, happier at that moment than I'd been in a long time. Both of my favorite males together, at least for this moment.

We settled at the kitchen table, and I ate two bowls of George's chili. It took a while because between bites I told him everything that had happened so far. I have a tendency to intentionally leave out facts when I tell a story, but this time, with George, he got the full text. We recorded our conversation on a fresh tape as a backup, in case anything happened to us. Neither of us wanted to think about what could happen.

George suggested putting the tape in the mail and sending it back to his house. That way we could use it as leverage, just like in the movies. And no one could get their mitts on it in the meantime.

George and I worked out a plan from the cushions of his leather sofa, side by side, holding hands and speaking in whispers while soft music played in the background. The drama of the situation made for heady sensations and impulses on my part. I kept glancing at George's muscles. He wore a white T-shirt, the sleeves riding just above his biceps.

I was sixty-six years old! Married to the same man for over forty years! I couldn't believe what was going through my mind. And through the rest of my body. Barney was my first and I thought he'd be my last.

"I'll drop the tape in the mail first thing tomorrow," George said. "You better stay out of sight and let me be your eyes and ears and legs."

I felt like I'd come home. To stop running and have three square meals a day, hanging out with George and Fred. I gave a big, contented sigh and could almost forget I was a hunted woman.

"You'll pick up Laura for me?" I asked. "So I can get some answers?"

George ran a finger down my arm, sending shocks of electricity through all the right places. Until now, I hadn't realized how much I missed a good man's touch. "I'll bring her to your doorstep," he said.

"I have a better idea," I said.

"You want me to bring her someplace else?"

Could I go through with it? Maybe we could keep the lights off so he couldn't see. I gulped. Then I remembered how George's wife had run off at Christmas time all those years ago, leaving a letter on the kitchen table. As far as I knew, he hadn't been with another woman since, not that I didn't understand. After what she did!

George might be just as nervous as I was. What if he said no? Shouldn't I wait for him to make the first move? Doubt crept into my thoughts. What was I doing?

If I thought about it much longer, I'd end up running out the door.

"Laura has nothing to do with my better idea," I said, standing up and leading him through the living room toward the bedroom. George scrunched his brow like he was trying to understand a foreign language without a single lesson. By the next look on his face, I knew he'd caught on to my plan. When he didn't pull back, I knew he approved.

All I'm saying about that night is that Fred slept on the floor.

The rest is between me and George.

THIRTY-ONE

WHEN I WOKE UP, George was gone. It was ten o'clock in the morning. I hadn't ever slept that long before. It must have something to do with the straw bed I had to sleep on Tuesday night, and … well … George and I hadn't slept much last night either.

I stayed in bed for awhile, replaying the night in my head, over and over like my minirecorder tape. What a man!

A fresh pot of coffee greeted me along with Fred. I let him out and he disappeared around the corner of the house at a trot, heading for an outbuilding. George is our local dog catcher, along with everything else he does. He rounds up strays and keeps them in roomy kennels in the outbuilding until he can find their old homes or new ones for them. Fred must have a new girlfriend out back to get him fired up like that.

More coffee, a shower, and I was set to go. George and I were meeting at noon with or without Laura in tow. The tape would be in the mail. After checking on Fred and finding him nose to nose with a cute Irish setter, I snuck off without him. He didn't mind at all. Last I saw, the two of them were wagging their tails like crazy. Fred's ears were at an awkward angle, slicked back with romance.

Love does crazy things! Don't I know it!

Close to my home, I left the road and drove through a field into the pines. When I was sure no one could see the truck, I parked and walked in to the deer blind Barney built years ago on our back forty.

We have so much land in the U.P. we referred to it in forty-acre parcels instead of single-acre lots. I have two forties left after giving a forty each to Blaze and Star. Heather, my Milwaukee-dwelling other daughter, didn't want anything to do with living in the woods, or I would have given her one, too. Maybe someday her son, Little Donny, will want it.

My hunting blind hadn't been used since November when deer hunting season ended. I used it as a retreat when my family got to be too much for me. I'd lay back in the La-Z-Boy with my feet up, listening to the crackle from the propane heater and watch deer come in to eat apples and corn I'd throw out for them.

It was a haven for me and for the deer. Shooting wild animals is a part of life here, a necessity for survival, since jobs are scarce and money is tight. But I let others take care of that. I couldn't look an animal in the eyes and then end its life.

Today, the going wasn't easy. In early spring, the ravines are marshy. I slopped through water up to my shins in some places before climbing to higher ground. The door to the blind squeaked when I opened it. I surveyed the inside of my mini home-away-from-home. Other than a few nuts stuffed into the corner of my chair and a couple flies buzzing at the window, nothing had changed in the last five months. I started the heater, hoping to dry out my pant legs.

George and Laura came walking in from the opposite end, right where I expected them. They'd missed the fun of tromping through the wetlands. I wished I'd thought of that.

I don't know how George got Laura to agree to meet, but she didn't have a weapon pointed at her back. She hadn't been physically coerced. I watched them approach and smiled. George looked great. Maybe that's why Laura came willingly. George used his sex appeal to bewitch her in the same way he'd lured me in. For a sixty-year-old, he was dynamite.

I gave George my favorite chair and opened two folding chairs for Laura and me. We sat down, my pant legs as near to the heater as possible without starting them on fire.

"George said it was important that we talk," Laura said. "I brought my recorder. Is this about another story?"

"Not exactly," I said. "You've had all the stories you're going to get."

"I'm really sorry the last one didn't run." Laura looked like a spring tulip, all rosy and fresh. "I'm still working on my boss."

"George," I said, hauling my stun gun out of my purse. "Will you watch for intruders while Laura and I have a little conversation?"

"Sure," he said, right on cue like we'd discussed last night. "But screams might be heard by somebody. Sound carries quite a distance in the woods." He looked at Laura. "No screaming."

"What are you talking about?" Laura said, eyeing George, then my weapon. From the look on her face I could tell she wasn't sure what it was.

I turned it on for effect.

"You said you lost my cattle prod," George said to me. It was the truth. I'd borrowed the prod from him and liked it so much, I kept it.

"I found it again," I lied, making my eyes into what I thought were dangerous slits. "Laura, I want to know why you were having an affair with Tony Lento. I want all the facts, every last one."

"What are you talking about?" Laura said with wide, innocent eyes. I almost believed she was innocent. She was that good. "I never met the man."

"But you know who I'm talking about?"

"Of course I do. I'm a reporter. His death was all over the news wires."

"My trigger finger is starting to tremble. This thing might get away from me." I moved toward her. She jumped up.

"You're crazy! I don't know what you're talking about. Touch me with that and I start screaming."

"No screaming," George warned from the door like he was telling a dog to stop barking.

"Look," Laura said. She had her cool back. "Let's work this out. Okay. Tell me why you think I was involved with Tony Lento."

So I did. She listened without interrupting me. Then she said, "I didn't have a conversation with you on the phone yesterday. I was in Munising on assignment. If you don't believe me, we can call the paper and verify it. I didn't know Tony Lento personally and I didn't give away your hiding spot. I didn't even know where you were."

"There's only one way to get the truth out of you," I said.

Laura was ready to fight me and my weapon. She still stood, tense and alert. "Sit down," I said, turning the stun gun off and re-

213

turning it to my purse before George could lay claim to it. "I have a truth serum. If you're innocent, you don't have a thing to worry about."

"I'm not drinking anything," Laura said, holding her ground.

"Nothing like that."

I made her repeat what she'd told me into the tape recorder, but I already knew the answer. Her voice, once I listened carefully to her, wasn't the same one I'd heard on the phone.

The tape confirmed it.

Once Laura realized the tables were turned, she let her indignation show, sputtering and complaining about false pretenses and physical threats. Maybe reporters in the U.P. don't get much of that, but they should be prepared for anything.

"I'm going to give you an exclusive," I said to appease her. "Once this case is solved, you get my story."

That quieted her down while she thought about the possibilities.

"I had to have been talking to Shirley on the phone," I said. "She lied to me, and I'm going to find out why."

"In the meantime," George said to Laura. "You need to be extremely careful."

"Don't be silly. I'm a big girl."

"Big men have been killed over this. Guns take down big girls, too," he argued. "And your roommate is right in the middle of something nasty."

"That's right," I said. "Shirley's up to something."

"If you think she was having an affair with a married man, you're wrong," Laura said. "She's not like that."

"Shirley had all of us fooled," I said. "She must be part of the gang. Is she still at your house?"

Laura nodded. "She's leaving for lower Michigan in the morning."

Before we left the hunting blind, George and I convinced Laura to keep quiet about our discussion, at least until we had time to talk to Shirley. But she refused to take any personal precautions, arguing that she had been safe until now. There was no reason to believe anyone would harm her. "Especially," she said, "not my friend Shirley."

From the tree line, we watched her drive away. I felt shy, self-conscious about last night. George must have felt the same because he had his eyes planted on the ground at his feet.

"Do you want to go back to being friends?" I asked.

"We never stopped." The snake on George's cowboy hat watched me.

"You know what I mean?" What if he regretted our hot, passionate night together? If this new twist on our relationship didn't work, could we go back to our easy friendship of yesterday? Somehow, I doubted it.

George's gaze lifted to me. "I had a wonderful time last night," he said. "I'm in for the long haul. How about you?"

I nodded, hiding my relief. The long haul for us could end any time, if Dickey spotted me. George wrapped his arms around my neck and pulled me close. "Cora Mae's home," he said.

I squealed. "She's sprung? What happened?"

"I called an attorney in Escanaba, and he worked out her release. Cora Mae's never been in trouble before, so they didn't consider her a flight risk."

"What about Blaze?"

"They're holding him in Escanaba. I stopped in at the jail. He's doing okay."

"And Kitty?"

"She isn't doing so well. The doctors discovered internal bleeding and had to take her back into surgery through the night. She's starting all over again in ICU with the same prognosis—wait and see."

I fought back tears. While George and I had been experimenting with a new beginning, Kitty was fighting against the end.

"There's more," George said while we drove in his truck to pick up mine.

I sighed, feeling tired. "What else?"

"When I drove past the gas station on the outskirts of Stonely, I spotted a carload of guys at the pumps. The one pumping gas had on orange shoes."

"The Orange Gang," I said. "What are they doing in Stonely? That's a long way from home."

"Why don't you go back to my place," George said. "I'll snoop around and see what I can come up with."

"Sounds good to me," I said, knowing he wouldn't be happy with my next move, if he found out. That's the thing with men. They like you the way you are, until you commit to them. Then they want to change you. They like control.

George drove off.

I headed for Gladstone to confront Shirley.

THIRTY-TWO

No one was home at Laura's house. I looked in all the windows. Nothing. Then I drove to the Dairy Flo, ordered a giant pop and a vanilla cone, and planted myself in front of the house on Dakota Avenue to wait.

Idling away the time gave me space to think.

Shirley had played a starring role since the moment the robbery went down. She'd been behind the counter and sounded the alarm. After that something happened to scare her into abandoning her home. She told me Tony was after her. But my minitape recorder proved she was having an affair with him. Had they been in it together? Had one of them double crossed the other?

I went over the robbery step by step, replaying the scene in my head. But I wasn't as young as I used to be. Keep at it, I said to myself. What did the robber do? What had he said?

He had threatened the line of customers, warning us that his partner was outside. Once he realized he was trapped, he swore and clunked Shirley, who was masquerading as Angie, on the head, knocking her out cold.

Why did he hit her? She'd already ruined his plan.

Light bulbs lit up in my head. I'd missed an important clue that had been right in front of my nose from the very beginning. During the robbery, I thought Kent Miller had been swearing. Well, he had. He'd said, crap. But then he said, Shi.... But he hadn't been starting a new cuss word. He was going to say the name of one of the members of his team. But he caught himself in time. Kent Miller was going to call out to Shirley once he realized that she had doublecrossed him by sending out for help.

Yes! I had my first direct tie-in between Shirley and the robbery, and I was excited.

Shirley had been part of the robbery! He knew who she really was, not Angie but Shirley.

I licked a circle around my ice cream cone, which was melting from lack of attention.

Okay, Kent, Shirley, and Bob were in it together. Shirley already had the money.

Wait. That wouldn't work. If Shirley had the money, why rob the bank? And why rob fake money? And why sound the alarm?

The only thing for certain was that Shirley had alerted the sheriff. She wanted the authorities to apprehend the robbers. That would lead to an investigation of the credit union's cash and the missing money would be discovered. A teller would know the sequence of events after any kind of robbery.

So Shirley wanted that to happen. Maybe she was setting up the entire gang to take the fall while she scooted off with the cash.

What a feat! Was she smart enough to point fingers at the two robbers and the inside thief, and walk away with the money?

I wiped ice cream from the front of my shirt with a paper napkin.

The inside thief. That's where Tony came into her plan.

I knew this was all speculation, but I'd had a lot of days on the run to figure it out. For now I didn't have to take care of Grandma or Blaze or cook meals or clean my house. The laundry didn't need doing because I didn't have any clothes to wash and I couldn't work my Trouble Buster business for obvious reasons. That left plenty of time on my hands to play with different scenarios.

Tony was having an affair with Shirley. He also had been at the hospital, asking the Orange Shoe guy for some kind of information, and he'd practically admitted the robbery and killing to me. He knew I was following him, so using my Glock to kill Bob Goodyear would have taken me out of the picture.

It sort of had.

I'd never heard of so many bad eggs in the same carton before. Bob, Kent, Shirley, and Tony, all smelling like rotten eggs. Mr. Tony Lento, pillar of Stonely society, had let lust destroy his comfortable rural life.

Tony and Shirley had been cozy in the woods, but something had happened to make Shirley run and hide. She claimed Tony was after her, trying to set her up. Maybe he wanted his share of the money. Maybe the orange shoes Shirley threw in the lake were hers. What if she had the money all along? Where would she hide it? And why was she still hanging around this neck of the woods?

I had so many more questions to answer, but the pop from the Dairy Flo was … well … flowing through me. I needed a bathroom quick, but Laura DeLand needed a better security system, because her back door lock sprung free on my first try. I put the fingernail file back in my purse and let myself in.

The house even sounded empty, if that's possible. After tackling my bladder problem, I wandered down a short hallway and found Shirley's room. Since she was in transition, there wasn't much to see. A few things hanging in the closet. A top dresser drawer with articles of clothing. It didn't take long to learn that she didn't have a hundred thousand dollars lying around inside Laura's spare bedroom.

When I peered through the front window to make sure the coast was clear, an old Cadillac with a bad muffler drove slowly past. Four punk types stared at the house through open car windows. I could see piercings and tattoos and ball caps flipped backward. The car eased down the street and turned left.

I ran for my truck, thinking they might come around again. If they stopped out front, I didn't want to be anywhere nearby. Too late, I heard the big car coming up behind Walter's truck. I slunk down, one eye peeled to the rearview mirror. They parked right behind me.

The two guys in the front got out. I flattened into the seat, grateful to be small. They walked past my side of the truck. I held my breath and made like a seat cushion.

"Ain't nobody around," I heard one of them say from the other side of Walter's rusted-out floorboards.

"What about that reporter chick?"

"I'ze tellin' you it's safe. Let's go."

They headed around the back of Laura DeLand's house. I couldn't help noticing they both wore orange sneakers and looked like Big Bad Leroy Brown, only bigger and badder.

I snuck another peek in the rearview mirror. Two more were in the back seat. At first I thought they were making out, they were so close together. Then I heard an angry raised voice. "I'll put your lights out," a guy said with menace.

Walter's bad truck body was turning into an asset. Better than a motorcycle for hearing outside conversation but without the visibility.

"I'm telling you, I don't have it," the other one said.

"Shut up."

The car went silent. But I'd heard enough.

Shirley was in the back seat of the old Cadillac and from what I'd overheard, she wasn't happy to be there.

A post office mail truck turned onto Dakota Avenue with its little flashing light mounted on the top. A female postal worker got out two doors down and strolled along the sidewalk leading to the house in front of her. She had a mailbag slung over her shoulder. She inserted a handful of letters into a mailbox mounted next to a neighbor's front door. When she arrived at Laura's house, she rummaged in her bag, pulled out a few letters, and left them in Laura's black mailbox. Before continuing her route, she tugged out a package about the size of a box of candy. It joined the other mail, but was too large for her to close the lid.

The mail carrier left it open and continued down the row of houses.

I almost gave myself away to the characters in the car behind me. The temptation to snatch the package almost overcame my common sense.

At last, I was pretty sure I knew exactly where the stolen money had gone.

I should have figured it out much earlier. Shirley was hanging around waiting for something she'd purchased on eBay. Yah, right. Had I seen a computer at her house? No, I hadn't. So how had she ordered through eBay? Didn't she need a computer and an Internet connection to do that?

Just as George and I had protected our tape recorded conversation by sending it to his house, Shirley had mailed the stolen money to herself at Laura's house. That woman was two steps ahead of me all the time.

Or she had been until the Orange Gang nabbed her.

I had to get my hands on that package before the punks from lower Michigan got hold of it.

But how?

THIRTY-THREE

I ZAPPED THE GUY in the back seat of the Cadillac before he knew what was coming. One hit, then two with my trusty stun gun, just to make sure he wouldn't give me any trouble. He flopped around half on the floor with both legs doing the turkey trot out the back door. I recognized him from the morgue. He was dead Bob's brother.

Shirley took the opportunity to grab his gun. I didn't think she was choosing my side of this war, so I gave her a zap, too, causing her to drop the weapon and join the dance. My aim hadn't been quite as good with her as it had been with the guy, but I didn't have time for a second round, if I wanted to get away in one piece.

I ran for the porch, grabbed the package from the mailbox, and beat it out of there as the other two Orange Gang members ran from the house. I slapped down the truck's door lock just in time and squealed away from the curb with one of them hanging onto the door handle. He dragged about a block before he decided it wasn't such a good idea and let go. My fully loaded, live-action stun gun aimed out the window helped him make the decision.

Walter's truck didn't have much zip, but I knew the territory, which I hoped would give me an advantage.

The Cadillac didn't have any guts either, because it didn't gain on me. It didn't lose either. I blew out of Gladstone, on the look-out for one of our law enforcement officials. If my luck held one would stop both vehicles and I'd be saved. I didn't see a squad car anywhere in sight. Where in the world are they when you really need them?

My plan, what little I had of one, was to drive to the Stonely jail and turn myself in along with the package addressed to … I forgot to look. There it was, clear as day. The package was addressed to Shirley Hess. Before I came in from the cold, I really should look inside. So, I worked on opening it while driving down Highway M35 as fast as possible.

The package was lighter than I'd expect one carrying that many bills to weigh. And I didn't really know how thick a stack of money would have to be to make up enough to spell out one hundred thousand. Was the package too small?

By the time I got it open, I had had several close calls with the shoulder of the road and the substantial ditches the U.P. is known for.

I dug inside the package and pulled out a handful of hundred dollar bills. I almost left the road again.

Holy Smokes! I thought I knew what I'd find, but really finding it threw me off for a minute. Somebody better be at the jail to help me before the Orange Gang arrived, hot on my tail.

Stonely came into my sights dead ahead and I tromped the gas harder even though my foot was already riding the floor and it didn't make a bit of difference in my speed. Wouldn't it be great if the Caddy chasers didn't realize they were turning into the sheriff's quarters, and they followed me right in? Dickey and I could round them up together. I'd be a hero and have a road named after me.

Right before town, I hear a voice speaking to me. I almost left the road again while I assessed its position. As much as I wished for it, the voice wasn't coming from Barney.

"Turn left at the next road," it said. I glanced sharply in my rear-view mirror. Shirley Hess' face was glaring at me through the back window from the bed of the truck. She had the gang member's gun pressed up against the glass, and her face meant business.

She must have dived into my truck while I was galloping for the mailbox. I should have taken the time for a second zap, but hindsight is always twenty-twenty, and my foresight has always been legally blind.

I peeled around the corner like she asked me to, turning more sharply than I needed to. I glanced back, hoping she had fallen out on the turn. She still clung there with a bead on my head.

"Make a left up ahead," she demanded, directing three more turns that were guaranteed to lose the Caddy, and which took me farther away from Stonely and the safety of the jail. I never had thought of it as a sanctuary until now.

"Where are we going?" I shouted through the glass, forgetting about the technology-advanced listening holes in the floorboards.

"Just drive." The gun never wavered. I don't know how I stayed on the road because my eyes were glued to the weapon and Shirley's trigger finger. A bad bump in the dirt road and I'd be a goner.

"If you reach toward your purse one more time," she said, "I'll shoot you right through the glass and take my chances without a driver."

She didn't miss a trick. Grandma's pistol was a foot away and it wasn't doing me any good at all.

We'd lost the Cadillac. I had a gun pointed at the back of my head. A hundred thousand dollars lay on the seat beside me. And there wasn't a soul in the world who knew where I was, or what I had discovered.

Shirley had a mean, violent streak. She'd plotted to steal the credit union's money for herself. She'd killed Tony and maybe Bob. If she would murder her lover, she wasn't going to worry about wasting me.

I needed to get to my purse-filled arsenal before we arrived at Shirley's destination. Because after that, I was a dead woman.

THIRTY-FOUR

LIKE I SAID BEFORE, I've lived in this area long enough to know the landscape just like I know the liver spots on the back of my hands, so I knew where we were going. I didn't like it. The bridge where Tony had crashed through on his way down to the Escanaba River loomed ahead.

It was the same place where Barney had gone fishing on his last day on earth.

One way to dislodge Shirley from her seat of power would be to take the same route Tony had, soaring out over the thirty-five foot drop-off, hoping I'd survive the fall. Shirley Hess would leave the truck whether she wanted to or not, and she'd take a solo dive into the rocky river below.

Had Tony died from head injuries or had he drowned? That would be good to know before I attempted the plunge.

"Pull over on the other side of the bridge," Shirley said from the back as we drew near.

An investigator has to be quick on her feet. Decisions have to be made in split seconds, even the life-or-death ones don't always wait for a convenient time. I aimed at the broken railing with sweat streaming down my temples and cold fear clutching my heart.

If only Barney would give me a sign, tell me if I was making a big mistake. But he kept silent, leaving me to make my own way.

Shirley realized what I was up to. A glance in the rearview mirror showed her startled face craning to see over the top of the truck. My driving skills were questionable on a good day, and this wasn't a good day. Could I pull it off?

Inches from the edge of the ledge, I jerked the steering wheel back toward the road and closed my eyes. One little misjudgment and the truck would go over sideways.

When I opened them, I was heading for the other side of the bridge. I had overcorrected and was now in jeopardy of going over the other side. I jammed the steering wheel the other way, pounding the brakes. Wheels screeched, I screamed, the truck skidded back the other way, its front bumper breaking through the railing on the same side as Tony's last launch, but in a new section a little farther down. The truck lurched to a stop with one of the front tires over the edge.

It was the first chance that I'd had to look in the back of the truck.

No Shirley.

I couldn't bring myself to look down into the abyss. Fear had frozen my body. A moan escaped from this steely investigator's throat, and I was relieved that no one was around to hear it, because it sounded more animalistic than human.

Did I mention that the river is way, way, way down below? And I was at a quandary again. If I got out of this alive, I didn't want to make another decision for a very long time. The question that had to be answered was this—should I slip the truck into reverse and try to back off the ledge onto the road? Or should I ease my body out? Would the shifting weight tip the truck over the edge?

I chose the second option, so I worked on my paralysis, moving my neck, then my arms. The package had landed next to me, but my purse was too far over to risk a reach. I didn't even turn the ignition off, just slid out with as little motion as possible. The truck held its position until I forgot to be careful in my relief to be on firm footing. I slammed the door. That little bitty slam caused Walter's truck to inch forward in what seemed like slow, groaning reluctant motion—like it had a mind of its own and didn't appreciate the direction it was taking.

Then it disappeared over the side of the road, flipping as it went. The noise when it hit the water was like the thunder of an ancient timber tree smashing to the earth. A tremor ran through the road beneath my feet.

I couldn't see Shirley anywhere down there in the swirling rapids. What if the truck had fallen directly on her?

Before I could get too upset over that image, I heard her voice calling for help from the opposite side of the road. She'd managed to grab a clump of brush when she ejected from the truck, but she was dangling in a dangerous position.

Right where I wanted her.

"Help me up," she croaked, trying to get leverage on her own.

"I'll help you after you answer a few questions," I said, watching her struggle. "If I don't like the answers, you'll have to drop and take your chances, because this way will be closed off to you."

A car drove toward the bridge. I leaned against the rail like a tourist and waved as it passed. The driver waved back and kept going.

"I can't hold on much longer."

"Than you better make your answers fast and truthful. First question, who's responsible for stealing the credit union money?" I glared at her.

"Tony stole the money and gave it to me for safekeeping. He wanted to run away with me. I'm going to fall."

"I'm already tired of asking questions. Why don't you tell me the whole thing?"

Shirley chanced a peek below and decided to cooperate. "We knew someone would catch on to the missing money eventually, so Tony thought we should set up a fake bank robbery. The robber would get away since I was working inside, and that would explain the disappearing funds. We'd be home free."

"But you're the one who sounded the alarm."

Shirley didn't look too comfortable. She'd managed to find a toe hold. The bush she clung to seemed to be supporting her weight. The river roared and bucked below.

"Let me up. I'll tell you everything."

"Keep talking." Neither of us had a weapon, but she was younger and stronger. I didn't want to get physical with her, because I'd lose.

"Tony was a fool. I didn't want him." She struggled a little, trying to change her position. Her arms had to be getting tired, because her words came faster. "I set it up with the Orange Gang and told them where to find the biggest bills in the vault. They didn't have a clue that they were stealing worthless paper. Tony made sure it was in perfect position."

"Then you turned on your partners, all of them, even Tony? You wanted the missing money discovered to get rid of Tony?"

"Only he caught on and came after me."

"Why did Bob kill Kent?"

"That wasn't part of the plan. No one was supposed to die."

"But Bob panicked."

"I'm getting a cramp in my hand."

"Who killed Bob? Did Tony?"

"Yes," she said, but I could see the lie in her eyes.

I picked up a stone the size of a quarter and aimed at her head.

"Okay, I did," she said, catching my intent. Where was my tape recorder when I needed it? "Bob wanted a bigger cut of the money after he killed Kent. He became a serious liability."

Unbelievable! This woman had set up a real robbery and a fake one, with the intention of leaving all her partners in crime for the lynch mob—Tony, Bob, and Kent.

"You killed Tony?"

"He found out what I was up to. He broke into my house. It was him or me."

I shook my head. Maybe I should let her take her chances in the Escanaba River. My Barney hadn't deserved to die at its hands, but I didn't feel the same conviction about her. The woman was pure evil.

"Who attacked the trailer and hurt Kitty?" I wanted to know.

"That wasn't me." She said it like that made all the difference in the world. At long last there was a malicious, violent act that couldn't be attributed to Shirley. "That was the Orange Gang."

"Why would the gang care about us? The Trouble Busters weren't involved."

She did that eye thing again.

"You told them we had the money. Didn't you?"

Shirley didn't answer, but I knew I was right. I watched another car approaching, kicking dust up in its wake. I would flag it down and ask for help. I stared down at the package of money, before moving back and letting Shirley struggle up. I had a fistful of small stones in my other hand in case she came at me.

"You're going to tell the truth when it comes time," I said. "No more lies."

She looked down the road. "Oh Gawd," she said, staring in terror at the oncoming car. When my eyes darted to see what was up, she broke into a run, heading in the opposite direction. Even with my running shoes on, I wouldn't catch her. But I had a plausible story and the package of money that had been delivered under her name. That didn't seem like as much evidence as I'd thought it was, but it was better than nothing.

Why didn't Shirley fight me for the money? It was as if she had forgotten all about it.

Then I heard the approaching car's bad muffler.

The Orange Gang had found us.

THIRTY-FIVE

SHIRLEY RAN AROUND THE side of the embankment, scrambling for the best way down to the river without breaking her neck. My reflexes weren't quite as fast, so the Orange Gang got me before I even made it off the road.

Bob's brother shoved me against the Caddy while the other two chased Shirley. I'd hidden the package down the front of my pants where it slid sideway, the edge jabbing me in the crotch. The gun in the punk's hand worried me more than a little physical discomfort. I'd also managed to pick up a few stones.

It was the best I could do. I used to have an arsenal of weapons. That was before the truck pitched from the cliff, taking my purse with it. Stones would have to do.

Based on the size of this guy's head though, the stones would be about as effective as raindrops.

"Where is it?" he said.

I knew better than to say, where's what? His eyes were cold like those of a bottom-feeding fish. "I threw it over the edge," I said.

I heard Shirley scream. A gunshot pierced the air below and I wondered if it had struck its target.

This whole country seems to think a handgun is more accurate than it really is. Unless you're a sharpshooter, with hours of practice under your belt, you'll discover that a moving target is hard to hit. A shooter's experience and the gun's accuracy have to be in perfect synch.

Common criminals like these dopes buy cheap guns to go with their small brains. My guy carried a Saturday night special that had less fire power and accuracy than Grandma Johnson's pathetic pistol.

So I took a chance. When my captor went to the railing to scan for the money and the source of the last shot, I clocked him in the head with my largest stone. I have a decent arm, considering all the years we'd had stone-skipping contests at this very river. I heard the thunk of it striking his head at the same time that he fired wildly in my direction.

At first, I didn't feel a thing. Then my left arm gave a shout of pain. Blood drops plopped on the ground beside me, while I stared at them in disbelief. A random careless shot and it struck me.

Bob's brother went down on his knees, holding his eye where the stone had made a direct connection with his eyeball. I ran around the other side of the Caddy. The punk raised his gun, squinting in my direction.

I needed a giant rock. Or a passing car. Or something. The next shot from him hit the Caddy and blew out a window. A zillion bits of shattered glass rained down on my head. I spotted a few loose chunks of concrete where Tony had bashed out the railing.

The Orange punk was wobbling on his feet. If I didn't hurry, his tiny mind might clear. My second shot with the clump of hardened cement missed completely, partially due to the pain in my injured arm. The third one hit its mark but didn't have enough velocity to do any harm. I didn't have any more fight left in me. I thought I was doomed, as I watched the chunk of concrete graze his thick arm.

Then his gun discharged. He screamed.

I've never seen anyone really shoot himself in the foot before, but it was a wonderful sight to behold. He hopped around while I assessed the hole in my arm and the amount of blood hitting the road. In the end it might turn out to be a flesh wound, but the amount of blood I was losing scared me almost to death.

The Cadillac driver had messed up big time, thinking he and his boys were infallible. He'd left the keys in the ignition. So while the big bad guy whimpered and nursed his little footsy, I started the car and drove off.

Let them figure out how to escape this one on foot.

A mile down the road, I met up with Dickey and George. Dickey was driving, which explained why I had to turn the big boat Caddy around and chase him. Then I had to almost run our acting sheriff off the road to get his attention.

Once I got it, George noticed my lifeblood draining out and talked Dickey into putting down the weapon he had trained on me.

"Follow me to the bridge," I shouted, one arm in the air in surrender, the other sopping with blood. "Wait until you see what's happening there."

George tried to stop me, yelling that he'd drive, but I didn't feel I had time to play musical chairs, so I took off. They followed.

The Orange Gang punk was waiting for his partners on the side of the road, right where I'd left him, still cradling his foot. For once, Dickey had the opportunity to draw on somebody other than me. He handcuffed the creep to the Caddy bumper.

George bandaged my arm while we waited for reinforcements and an ambulance. We didn't see Shirley or the other two gang members from where we stood. Several hours later, they pulled Shirley out of the Escanaba River, where she was shriveled up from the cold water, but still alive.

It turned out that the bad guys couldn't swim, so she weathered it out in the cold water, while the Orange Gang ran up and down the shoreline, taking pot shots.

And last, but not least, I pulled the package containing the hundred thousand dollars out of the front of my pants and presented it to Dickey, who took all the credit for recovering it when the news trucks showed up that evening at the jail.

I don't remember much about the ride into the Escanaba hospital. I recall the stretcher and strong arms securing me with straps. The loss of blood must have made me woozy, but I have a vivid image of George in the back of the ambulance with me, holding my hand and whispering comforting words.

Barney was there, too.

My husband had watched from the sidelines while the ambulance people worked, preparing me for the trip into Escanaba. He had a loving smile on his face, and at first I thought he was happy because I was finally joining him, wherever he was.

But he shook his head at that. "It's not time yet," he said. "It's going to take more than a shot in the arm to do you in."

"I'm real tired," I whined.

Later, George told me the three of us had quite a conversation on the way to the hospital.

I guess Barney gave George the okay. At least, that's what George said. When I'm well, I'll ask Barney about that. Having his approval would mean all the difference in the world.

After that, I slept.

THIRTY-SIX

Word for the Day
Peripatetic (per' i puh TET ik) adj.
Walking or moving about; not staying in one place.

AFTER I WAS RELEASED from the hospital, I gave sweet Laura De-
Land an exclusive, behind-the-scenes interview that was sure to
win her a newspaper prize. Then I drove over to the Escanaba
River, sat down on a rock, and made my peace with the river that
had claimed my husband. Those rapids had been an important
part of our lives, and it had given Barney years of happiness fighting trout on the end of his fishing line.

It was time to forgive it.

My arm was bandaged and cradled in a sling, making driving
difficult. I'd been warned by the doctors to stay out from behind
the wheel, but I'd never taken anyone's advice before and it was
too late in my life for me to start listening now.

Walter had understood about the demise of his truck. "You've destroyed every vehicle you've ever driven," he said. "What does this make? Three? I wasn't expecting to get it back in one piece."

I didn't even have to apologize for the bullet-ridden condition of his trailer. George would replace a few windows and it would be just as good as anything else Walter owned.

Blaze was doing well, back at home with Mary, worrying about the mess Dickey must be making of the town's law enforcement. So he's recovering. The family expects some ups and downs. I don't want to be the one to tell Blaze that he might not be up to sheriffing ever again, that retirement came earlier than he expects. All he used to talk about was retiring, now all he cares about is getting back to work.

If nothing else, he can join the Trouble Busters. We could use a former law officer on the team.

The river brought back some good memories. I closed my eyes and heard my kids laughing and running along the bank, skipping stones and dipping bamboo poles in between the rocks hoping for a hit. We had a wicker creel basket filled with rainbow trout that I liked to pan fry after rolling them in a flour and cornmeal mix.

I stood up and gave the river one last look before heading home.

Fred came running to greet me when I pulled into my driveway. The guinea hens flapped angrily behind him just like always. Cora Mae and Kitty arrived and we took a slow walk down the road like the doctors advised for Kitty's recovery.

"I missed the whole darn thing," she said, walking slow as a turtle. "I could have been a big help."

"I was in jail through most of it," Cora Mae told her. "Poor Gertie. You had to solve the case all by yourself."

"The Trouble Busters will be back in business soon," I said. "You'll have lots of time for adventures. Right now we have to recover our strength by being peripatetic." My eyes slid over to Kitty. This was the test to see how well she really was.

Kitty, shuffling along in the middle, smiled and put one arm around Cora Mae and the other over my shoulder. "We're a chockablock team," she said. "We can surmount any acme."

I pretended like I understood her by nodding my head and smiling back. I wondered where I'd left my dictionary. I'd need it, if she was this good while she was still recovering.

When we got back to the house, Pearl was inside with Grandma Johnson, helping her get ready for Tony Lento's funeral.

"Which hat should I wear?" Grandma said, trying to chose between two old lady hats.

"The blue one goes best with your hair," Pearl offered.

"Don't let that dog in the house," Grandma shouted at Kitty, who was the last one coming in. My mother-in-law had resumed her position of power. "And, Gertie, don't mess up the kitchen while I'm gone."

Grandma Johnson and I were back to our constant battle over kitchen dominance, but it felt good to have everyone together again, even with all their quirks.

And later George was coming over for a sauna and whatever else came to mind.

Grandma plopped the blue hat on her head and was almost out the door, when she turned back. "I almost forgot. I'm so used to your wild ways and me an old woman."

"What now?" I asked.

"Blaze called while you were out for your walk. The sheriff's truck was pulled out of Thunder Lake."

I'd forgotten all about that truck. But Walter had done the deed, not me.

"Your fingerprints are all over it," Grandma continued, watching me with beady, knowing eyes.

"That's impossible," I said, cool and calm, with the authority and experience that comes with owning your own private eye business. Underneath my hard exterior, I was sweating bullets, trying to figure out if fingerprints could really stick to a vehicle if it was submerged.

"He's fighting mad, right along with Dickie Snell," Grandma said, clacking her false teeth. "Wouldn't surprise me if they showed up with a warrant for your arrest. He wants his Glock back, too."

After Grandma Johnson and Pearl pulled away and Kitty and Cora Mae drove off in the other direction, I packed a few belongings, called my dog, and ran for the woods.

RECICPES

YELLOW PEA SOUP

Pea soup is one of the oldest traditional dishes in Sweden, dating back to the Viking times. Grandma Johnson makes it with pig's feet, but I like to use ham hocks. Serve it with a dessert of Swedish pancakes, topped with preserves. Wash down with beer.

Serves four

    2 cups dried yellow peas

    2 quarts water

    2 ham hocks

    1 large onion, chopped

    1 bay leaf

    Salt

    Pepper

    Thyme

    Marjoram

    Mustard

In a big pot, soak the peas in the water overnight. Add everything else except the mustard. Cook for one hour or until the peas are soft. Scrape the meat from the hock. Add more water if the soup is too thick. Serve with mustard on the rim of the soup bowl.

TAFFY

We always had great fun pulling taffy. Ours is even better than the stuff they sell on Mackinac Island. We didn't have a candy thermometer when my kids were young. We sized it up the old fashioned way, by dropping a small dab into cold water and rolling it around to see if it formed a soft ball. You'll get the hang of it.

1 bottle white corn syrup

1 cup sugar

1 tsp vanilla

Boil the corn syrup and sugar until it forms a soft ball when a small amount is dropped into cold water. Add vanilla. Pour into a buttered pan and cool it just enough to handle it. Butter your hands. Pull until it's white and stiff. The taffy can be divided into pieces so everyone can pull. When done, pull into long ropes, let it harden on waxed paper, and cut it into pieces with scissors.

Note: Make butterscotch taffy by using dark corn syrup instead of white.

POTATO SAUSAGE

We all own grinders with ½-inch stuffing attachments. Don't you? If not, you'll have to find a Yooper and borrow the equipment. You can get sausage casings in the meat department at your favorite grocery store.

1 pound ground pork
2 pounds ground venison
1 pound ground beef
6 potatoes, finely ground
2 onions
1 tsp allspice
Salt
Pepper
1 package sausage casings

Mix all ingredients, stuff with grinder attachment. Drop the sausages into boiling water. Cook for 30 minutes.

If you enjoyed reading *Murder Talks Turkey* by Deb Baker,
read on from a new Kate London Mystery by Susan Goodwill:

Little Shop of Murders

ONE

"I'LL BET MERCURY's IN retrograde, Kate." My Aunt Kitty London's stage whisper echoed through the lobby of Mudd Lake Savings Bank. "This town's crawling with crazy people and drunks."

I ran a hand through my unruly auburn curls and tried to sound calm. "The annual Sausage Festival always attracts a weird crowd," I said.

"Never do business when Mercury's in retrograde." Kitty fidgeted from one high-heeled ankle boot to the other. "That's what Roland says, and he's an excellent astrologer."

Kitty craned her neck around a beefy guy in a baseball cap and a *Flaming Sausage* jacket. I craned with her. At the counter, our teller doled twenties into the palm of a well-dressed man with a blond ponytail.

"This woman is entirely too slow," Kitty said, her voice louder this time.

The teller, whose nametag read Chiffon, frowned and arched an eyebrow in our direction. She restarted her count.

"Let's just keep a low profile until we get this money deposited."

I pressed the bag full of the town's money tighter to my side and eyed my seventy-five-year-old aunt in her faux fur vest, leather mini, and tights—her whole outfit in shades of purple God never put on a grape. Platinum curls poked out from beneath her tasseled Shriner's fez, and dangly purple star earrings reached almost to her shoulders. It'd been forty-odd years since her last movie, but she was the closest thing Mudd Lake had to a celebrity.

Low profile might be asking a lot.

"What if Fred changes his mind about our loan?" Kitty's voice went up a notch. "If the planets are out of alignment, Fred could change his mind. Should I call Roland? Maybe Psychic Buddies? I think I have them on speeddial." She dug in her fanny pack for her phone.

"Shh! Did you go off decaf again?" I whispered. I glanced around for Fred Schnebbly, the banker who held the London family's fate in his pencil-pushing hands. His office sat dark and unoccupied. "Fred said to make our deposits, then to see him and sign the papers."

Our extremely amateur theatre group, the Mudd Lake Players, had already made it through several surprising hoops—a fundraiser, a decent cast, even renting professional-grade alien plant puppets for the upcoming show.

After the loan, maybe we could jump through that last fiery ring, but it was a doozy. With a disaster-free opening night, we could wow the CracklePops Foundation and get that theatre restoration grant.

A disaster free opening night.

The planets had better be lined up like billiard balls for this thing to come off.

I scanned behind the counter for Fred and resisted my own fidgety urges. Just our teller and one other, more familiar face behind the counter: Patrice Stikowski.

Kitty zoomed in on Patrice, who counted and stacked bills behind a "Next Window" sign.

Kitty hoisted her tote bag high. "Halloo, Patrice!" she trilled. "Be a dear and wait on us. I've got five thousand dollars from the theatre benefit. It's making me quite nervous. Plus, Kate's got all the town's cash from the Sausage Festival." She jerked a thumb at my satchel.

I gazed at the high ceiling and sighed.

"Is that okay?" Patrice sent a questioning look to Chiffon. "Can I open up?"

The spring sunlight glinted off Patrice's new eyebrow rings, and her hair, dyed a conservative new-bank-teller-black, made her look like a Goth version of Snow White.

"You're not to open until Rhonda gets in." Chiffon huffed and slapped a stack of twenties on the counter. "I can't imagine where that girl has gotten to."

I sent Patrice a grin. "Thanks for trying."

"We theatre people have to stick together, you know?" Stick came out "thick" around her oversized tongue stud.

Kitty reached in her bag and pulled out a rolled up poster. She unfurled it to reveal a picture of a giant, snaggle-toothed, man-eating-alien-plant. Underneath, the words "Little Shop of Horrors, opening May 25th, at Mudd Lake's historic Egyptian Theatre" seemed to drip blood.

Kitty waved the poster at Chiffon. "Might we put this in the win—"

The door behind us whacked against the wall, and we all jumped. A whoosh of breezy Lake Michigan air blew past us, and a stooped, balding man in a red plaid bathrobe and floppy slippers burst into the lobby. He scuttled past us to the counter.

I guessed him to be about eighty years old. I smiled and leaned toward Kitty. "Sausage Festival fallout."

The geezer slipped around the pony-tailed man at the front of our line. He swiveled toward us, and shoved his hand in his bathrobe pocket. An outline of something jabbed out through the flannel.

My smile evaporated, and my heart slammed against my ribcage. A gun?

My throat tightened, and I grabbed Kitty's hand and squeezed.

"Everybody keep calm," the old man rasped. He hacked phlegm from his throat and swiveled to Chiffon. He pulled a crumpled IGA bag from his left bathrobe pocket and kept his other pocket low, below the counter. "This is a holdup."

Chiffon flicked a curtain of beaded cornrows over her shoulder and put one fist on her hip. She shoved the grocery bag back toward the old man and wagged a very long, very fake, green and white fingernail at him. "We're too busy for this today, Walter."

The elderly man took his hand from his pocket and cupped it to his ear. "Eh?"

My heart thudded as I watched, helpless. Chiffon hadn't seen the gun, I was sure of it.

The teller leaned over and raised her voice. "Did you get a new prescription or something?"

"What the—?" He stomped a floppy-slippered foot. "Dang it, Chiffon, of all the times to be a pain in the butt, this ain't it. Do what I say!"

"Nuh-uh. You go on home." She brushed her hand at him. "Shoo!"

He shifted his frail frame and planted his own hands on his hips. Chiffon grabbed a chocolate-frosted doughnut from a Krispy Kreme box behind the counter and chomped off a hunk. She glared at Walter while she chewed. The two spent several long seconds locked in a standoff. No one in the bank moved.

Frozen in place, I stared at the gun-shaped object sagging in Walter's bathrobe pocket. The sound of my own heart pounded in my ears.

I poked my head up to make contact with Chiffon. I tried pointing to the pocket with my eyeballs.

No response.

I jerked my head in the pocket's direction. I stretched my eyelids wide and mouthed the word "gun."

Chiffon looked over the robber's shoulder and frowned. "You got a problem, lady?"

Walter spun around, shoved his hand back in his pocket, and glared at us. I snapped my jaw shut and made my face a blank. I squeezed Kitty's bony hand tight.

"It'll be okay," Kitty whispered, her voice very quiet.

The old man looked at Kitty, then at me. He turned back to Chiffon. Out of the corner of my eye, I watched Patrice ease her hand toward the edge of the counter. I held my breath and waited.

Walter swished his pocket into view, exposing blue-and-white-striped pajama bottoms. He pointed his pocket at the scabby double rings in Patrice's newly-pierced left eyebrow.

"You! Away from the alarm. You want another hole in your fool head?"

Patrice let her hand fall and swallowed hard. Chiffon's eyes grew large. The last of her doughnut dropped to the floor.

"He's got a gun? He's got a gun? He's never got a gun." She stuck her arms in the air. "Help!"

Keeping his pocket pointed at Chiffon, Walter pushed the grocery bag back across the metal counter. Mudd Lake is a small town, and I'd never noticed until now that our teller windows were wide open—no bulletproof glass.

"Give me all your twenties," he said.

Chiffon dug in her cash drawer. She grabbed banded stacks of twenty-dollar bills and dropped them into the bag. "God, Walter, are you nuts?"

I hiccupped.

Uh-oh," Kitty whispered. "Try holding your breath."

Hic.

"It doesn't help," I said.

"I know," she whispered. "How're you going to be a law enforcement official, if you get the hiccups all the time when you're scared?"

"Shhh," I said and hiccupped again.

The man with the ponytail moved closer to Walter.

"And you," Walter spun around and shoved his gun pocket into the man's chest. "Back off!"

Walter snatched the wad of cash from the pony-tailed man's fist. The man's empty hand hung in the air for several seconds before it fell to his side.

Walter turned back to Patrice.

I wished I knew what to do. Three weeks as an auxiliary deputy, and so far I'd only done crowd control and pooper-scoop tickets.

"I want all your twenties. Every one of 'em!"

Patrice's eyebrow rings tinkled as she yanked money from her drawer. The old man looked around nervously.

Kitty lifted her free arm and wiggled her fingers in a wave. I hiccupped and jerked her hand. I clutched my satchel and tried not to move my lips.

"Don't draw attention to us," I whispered.

Too late.

The robber squinted at Kitty. He flashed a mouth full of oversized dentures in our direction and pulled his gun hand out of his pocket. He wiggled his fingers back.

Kitty smiled tentatively and batted purple eyelashes in Walter's direction. I stifled a groan. Kitty'd had seven husbands for a reason. She was a hopeless flirt.

The bandit's attention moved from Kitty to the swarthy guy in the *Flaming Sausage* jacket who stepped closer to Kitty. He put a meaty hand on her shoulder and in a thick European accent said, "Hey buddy, we want no troubles. Just do your job."

Walter squinted at him, then rammed his hand back in his pocket and whirled. He swooped his gun-pocket at Patrice. "Hurry the hell up!"

Patrice tossed her stack of bills to Chiffon, who loaded them in the paper bag and slid it across the counter. The old man snatched it and headed for the door. He stopped in front of us.

I clutched Kitty's hand, pressed the satchel to my side, and hiccupped. My heart banged like a snare drum in my ears.

"What's in those bags?" he said. He took a step forward.

Kitty jutted her chin and squeezed her tote bag to her chest. "None of your beeswax, Walter," she said.

I moved in front of her.

"You ladies got cash?" Walter wrapped bony fingers around the strap of my satchel.

My heart slammed a rhythmic message. *Do something, do something.* I thought of that gun, the people around us, Kitty right beside me. A sinking feeling took over, and I let him pull the satchel from my grasp.

He peered at Kitty. "Hey Kitty, is that the theatre money?"

"Let him have it," I whispered and hiccupped.

Kitty must have misunderstood because she stepped around me and whipped the bag in a wide arc. She walloped Walter full in the head with five thousand dollars in tens, twenties, and miscellaneous loose change.

"Aack!" Walter staggered back a step. The IGA bag and my satchel stayed under one arm and when Walter yanked his gun hand out to grab for his head, a banana flew from his bathrobe pocket.

My jaw unhinged, and I stared at the floor. A banana? A *banana*?

"No!" My breath escaped in a whoosh, and I lunged.

Walter rocked backward, took another step to steady himself, and stepped on the banana. It squished out of its skin and sailed past my left ankle.

Walter leapt at Kitty and ripped her tote bag free. She pitched forward, going in like the world's most diminutive, platinum-haired quarterback on a loose ball.

A flash of Kitty with a broken hip blazed before me. I thrust out my arm and snatched a fistful of faux-bunny. Keeping a tight hold, I swiped for the three bags with my free hand. Walter jerked backward, circled

around us, and setting some sort of old-fart-in-pajamas land speed record, sprinted to the exit.

I let go of Kitty, and she hotfooted it across the lobby.

The guy in the sausage jacket, the pony-tailed man, and I all bolted
for the door. Kitty got there first. She stood in the doorway.

"Walter, you're a rat's patootie!" she hollered.

A flash of plaid flannel disappeared around the corner one building
away.

"You know that guy?" I said, staring after it.

"You bet I do, the jackass!" Kitty said. "I'm dating him."

WWW.MIDNIGHTINKBOOKS.COM

From the gritty streets of New York City to sacred tombs in the Middle East, it's always midnight somewhere. Join us online at any hour for fresh new voices in mystery fiction, book club questions, author information, mystery resources, and more.

Midnight Ink promises a wild ride filled with cunning villains, conflicted heroes, hilarious hazards, mind-bending puzzles, and enough twists and turns to keep readers on the edge of their seats.

MIDNIGHT INK ORDERING INFORMATION

Order by Phone:

- Call toll-free within the U.S. and Canada at 1-888-NITEINK (1-888-648-3465)
- We accept VISA, MasterCard, and American Express

Order by Mail:

Send the full price of your order (MN residents add 6.5% sales tax) in U.S. funds, plus postage & handling to:

> Midnight Ink
> 2143 Wooddale Drive, Dept. 0-978-7387-1225-3
> Woodbury, MN 55125-2989

Postage & Handling:

Standard (U.S., Mexico, & Canada). If your order is:
$24.99 and under, add $3.00
$25.00 and over, FREE STANDARD SHIPPING

AK, HI, PR: $15.00 for one book plus $1.00 for each additional book.

International Orders (airmail only):
$16.00 for one book plus $3.00 for each additional book

Orders are processed within 2 business days. Please allow for normal shipping time.
Postage and handling rates subject to change.

ABOUT THE AUTHOR

Deb Baker grew up in the Michigan Upper Peninsula with the Finns and Swedes portrayed in *Murder Talks Turkey*. She has an intimate knowledge of the life and people of the region.

She lives in North Lake, Wisconsin, with her husband, two teenagers, two dogs, and two cats.

Visit Deb at www.debbakerbooks.com.